Book Four

EPIC ZERO 4

Tales of a Total Waste of Time

By

R.L. Ullman

Epic Zero 4: Tales of a Total Waste of Time

Cover design by Yusup Mediyan
All character images created with heromachine.com.

Published by But That's Another Story… Press
Ridgefield, CT

Printed in the United States of America.

First Printing, 2018.

ISBN: 978-0-9984129-4-8
Library of Congress Control Number: 2018913478

For Lucy,
the original Gray Ghost

Don't Miss the Epic Adventure!
From Award-Winning Author
R. L. ULLMAN
EPIC ZERO
TALES OF A NOT-SO-SUPER 6th GRADER
R. L. ULLMAN
EPIC ZERO 2
TALES OF A PATHETIC POWER FAILURE
R. L. ULLMAN
EPIC ZERO 3
TALES OF A SUPER LAME LAST HOPE
R. L. ULLMAN
EPIC ZERO 4
TALES OF A TOTAL WASTE OF TIME
R. L. ULLMAN
EPIC ZERO 5
TALES OF AN UNLIKELY KID OUTLAW
R. L. ULLMAN
EPIC ZERO 6
TALES OF A MAJOR META DISASTER
GET MORE EPIC!
Grab a FREE copy of
Epic Zero Extra only
at rlullman.com
R. L. ULLMAN
EPIC ZERO
Extra
TALES OF A SUPERHERO SCREW UP

TABLE OF CONTENTS

ONE

I TANGO WITH A T-REX

There's a rabid T-Rex on my tail.

Yep, you heard me. A gigantic, kid-eating Tyrannosaurus rex is stomping through Keystone City, and he's penciled me in for his next meal! Yeah, I know what you're thinking. How does a super-smooth hero like me always end up in ridiculous situations like this?

Honestly, I have no idea. But I guess it comes with the territory. After all, sometimes a hero's gotta do what a hero's gotta do. Even if he'd rather be doing *anything* else—like algebra or going to the dentist.

I hang a right at the corner bakery and make a beeline for Keystone Police Station. Why the police station? Well, it's not because I'm trying to stuff this Godzilla wannabe into a human-sized jail cell. That's impossible, although it sure would be nice.

No, I'm heading for the police station because that's where TechnocRat told me to meet him. He said he had a big solution for our not-so-little problem. And he better be right, because we're coming in fast, so I hope he's ready to deliver on his end of the deal.

THUMP!

My feet fly off the pavement. Every time that over-sized lizard takes a step, it's like a mini-earthquake throwing me off balance. But I can't stop now. I mean, I've seen all the Jurassic Park movies. I know exactly what'll happen if that thing catches up to me.

I slide across the front hood of an abandoned car. The only good news here is that the city was evacuated hours ago. That means there's no one crazy enough to be traipsing around town in this dangerous situation.

Well, present company excluded.

Suddenly, a hear a SWISH.

Instinctively, I duck just as a telephone pole whizzes over my head and punctures the street like a giant spear.

Now he's throwing things?

Just. Freaking. Wonderful.

Maybe he should be called a 'T-Wrecks?'

Bad puns aside, there was one little snag to our plan. In order to seal the deal, TechnocRat said he had to go back to the Waystation to get what he needed. You know, our secret headquarters way up in (gulp!) outer space.

So, yeah, I'm hoping he makes it back in time.

I hit Main Street and keep on booking. I can see the police station in the distance. It's a straight shot from here, probably six long blocks away. I'm winded, but if I stop to catch my breath, I'm toast.

Speaking of toast, I wonder what Dog-Gone's up to? When TechnocRat asked for a volunteer, that mutt stepped four paws backwards, basically leaving me on my own. So much for man's best friend!

And unfortunately, it's not like the rest of the Freedom Force are around to help. They're handling their own dinosaur problems all over the globe.

Dad and Makeshift are stopping a squad of Velociraptors marching through Mexico. Shadow Hawk and Blue Bolt are halting a herd of Ticeratops in Tokyo. Master Mime is wrangling a Megalodon in the Atlantic Ocean. And Grace and Mom are fighting a gaggle of Pterodactyls in Europe—try saying that one three times fast!

So, that leaves TechnocRat, Dog-Gone, and yours truly to take down this dino-sore right here in Keystone City. Which would have been a whole lot easier if the T-Rex was a Meta and I could simply negate his powers. But he's not, which means I'm powerless against him.

Not a great feeling.

We're three blocks away.

That rat better not let me down.

ROOAARR!

The hairs on the back of my neck stand on end. Peering over my shoulder, all I see are teeth—giant, super-sharp teeth! He's right behind me!

Time to motor! But I've been running for so long I'm losing—

SMACK!

Suddenly, I slam into something solid and find myself sitting on my backside. My nose is throbbing, and I wipe it with my sleeve. It's bloody. Marvelous.

What happened?

That's when I realize I'm staring at a pair of dark, green boots. But I thought the city was evacuated?

"Who are you?" comes a frantic voice.

Who am I? Sheesh, I really need to hire an agent. I look up to find a man staring at me with wild, brown eyes. He's wearing a cone-shaped helmet and a green jumpsuit with an hourglass insignia on his chest. I know I've seen his Meta profile before, but I can't place him.

Then, it clicks.

"You're the Time Trotter!" I say.

The Time Trotter is a Meta 1 villain with a magical watch that gives him the ability to travel through time. He's mostly a small-time crook who likes to pop up in history where he can profit the most—like when he stole the first truckload of gold headed for Fort Knox. He's had countless run-ins with the Freedom Force, but every time we're about to catch him he slips away through the timestream.

"Y-You're wearing a costume," he says, sounding strangely desperate. "Are you a hero?"

"The name's Epic Zero," I say, getting to my feet and dusting myself off. Even though I've single-handily saved the world three times, why is it that no villain has ever heard of me? "I'm on the Freedom Force."

"The Freedom Force!" he says, grabbing the front of my uniform. "Please, help me! I'm in danger!"

"Whoa, back off, buddy," I say, knocking his hands off the merchandise. "What danger?"

Then, I remember the T-Rex.

Where's the freaking T-Rex?

I glance over my shoulder to find the behemoth leaning over me, jaws wide open for the kill. I jump, but the T-Rex doesn't move. It's like he's … frozen?

"Don't worry," the Time Trotter says. "I've isolated time around him so that every second is moving a million times slower. I-I can do that now."

Wow, that's how I feel whenever Grace opens her mouth. But something's wrong. In the Meta Profile I read, the Time Trotter can only manipulate time around himself. It never said anything about him manipulating time for others. But if he can do that, then…

"Um, you wouldn't happen to be the one responsible for bringing all of these dinosaurs here, would you? Because as far as I can remember, you can't do that."

"I-I didn't think I could either," he says, talking

rapidly, "until he made me do it. But it hurts so much I-I can't bring any more."

"Whoa," I say. "Slow down. First off, who's this 'he' you're talking about?"

"Please," he begs. "I don't have time. The connection was severed, but I don't know for how long. Get me out of here. He's coming for me!"

"I'll try one more time," I say. "Who is 'he?'"

FWOOM!

Without warning, something powerful blows me backwards, throwing me to the ground. I land hard on my left shoulder, but that's the least of my problems. Because hovering above us is the giant head of a man!

But it's no ordinary man. This guy has red skin, pointy ears, and three orange eyes! I drop into a fighting stance, but then the man's face flickers and I realize he's not actually here. He's an image being projected from somewhere far away.

"No!" the Time Trotter screams, totally freaked out.

I study the red guy's face, but I don't recognize him.

"Time Trotter," the three-eyed man rumbles, his deep voice rattling my bones. "The distance is great, but I have restored our link. Yet, you disappoint me. I did not offer you a kingdom only to watch you play with toddlers."

Hang on. Did he just call me a toddler?

"P-Please," the Time Trotter pleads, holding his head in his hands. "I can't bring any more. It's too painful."

"I am afraid it is too late to renegotiate our bargain,"

the three-eyed man says. "You have a job to do. Now where is the Key?"

"I-I don't know," the Time Trotter says. "I can't find it. None of them can find it. Look, I'm sorry, I don't want a kingdom anymore. Just leave me alone. Please…"

"Enough!" the three-eyed man commands. Then, the eye in the middle of his forehead turns green. "I enhanced your power. But clearly, I erred in putting my trust in you, for I see you have already failed me. Your world's champions have already stopped your prehistoric pets before they could locate the Cosmic Key."

The Cosmic Key? What's that?

"It's not my fault," the Time Trotter pleads. "They're the Freedom Force. They're heroes."

"When I rule the universe," the man says, his third eye transforming back to orange, "there will be no more heroes. Or failures."

"Please!" the Time Trotter begs. "I-I'll ignore the pain. I'll go back in time and get more dinosaurs to search for the Cosmic Key. I-I can—"

"Silence!" the three-eyed man orders. "At least your creatures are more disciplined than you. They have spread far and wide across your pathetic planet, allowing me to conduct a proper scan. And while I no longer detect the presence of the Cosmic Key, I do sense its latent energy. It was here at one time but has since been removed."

Okay, this is getting weird. And why is he so determined to find this key?

"I imagine my greatest enemy is laughing at me now," the red man says. "He probably believes he has tricked me. He is probably expecting me to begin searching the universe anew. But the final laugh will be mine. For with your unique powers, we will indeed 'go back in time,' just as you suggest, and we will find the Cosmic Key on this very planet—before it was removed! Isn't that right my loyal subject?"

Then, the man's third eye turns green again.

"No!" the Time Trotter begs, but before he can run away, his body goes rigid and his eyes emit a faint green light. "Yes, master."

Master? Is he being mind controlled? I've got to—

But before I can act, there's a huge flash of white light and I'm blinded. It takes several seconds to stop seeing stars, but when I do the Time Trotter and his three-eyed friend have vanished. But if the Time Trotter is gone, does that mean—

CHOMP!

The T. Rex!

Suddenly, I'm lifted into the air, my legs dangling above the ground. My costume tightens around my neck, strangling me. I can't breathe! The T. Rex is reeling me into his mouth by my cape!

I've got seconds to act. I reach into my utility belt, pull out my pocket knife, and begin sawing away at the fabric of my cape. As the left side gives way, I feel something slimy run across the back of my neck! Was that his tongue? So gross!

I move into overdrive, frantically cutting away the right side of my cape until I rip through and drop to the ground. I hit the pavement feet first and let my forward momentum carry me into a somersault. If I survive this, I'll have to thank Shadow Hawk for teaching me that one.

I pop up and start running, my knees feeling like jelly.

STOMP!

He's chasing me again!

I'm two blocks from the police station.

Up ahead I see movement on the front steps. There's good old Dog-Gone prancing back and forth. And next to him is a tiny, white dot scampering over a gray object.

It's TechnocRat! He made it back!

And it looks like he's got his solution all right. It's some kind of a contraption, but why's he jumping off of it? If I didn't know better, I'd say he's looking for something on the ground—like he's lost something?

O. M. G! He's not ready!

One block away.

Suddenly, the area around me darkens, which can only mean one thing—the T-Rex is on top of me!

"Shoot it!" I yell.

"I need a second!" TechnocRat shouts back. "Stall!"

Stall? Are. You. Freaking. Kidding. Me?

Fifteen feet away.

"Hit it!" I yell.

"I can't," TechnocRat yells, "I'm missing a screw!"

"Darn right you're missing a screw!" I yell. "Shoot it! Blast it! Do something high-tech to it!"

Five feet away.

The T-Rex is nearly on top of me!

"Found it!" TechnocRat says, proudly holding up a silver screw in his pink paw. Then he looks my way and whispers, "Holy guacamole."

I look up to find humungous, razor-sharp teeth over my head. Newspaper headlines flash before my eyes: *Unknown Superhero Kid Swallowed by Hungry Dinosaur.*

The T-Rex closes his mouth.

"Auuuuuuugh!" I scream, diving to the ground.

VZOOM!

A neon green beam shoots straight over my head and slams into the dinosaur. The creature staggers backwards, caught in a dazzling vortex of green energy. The T-Rex ROARS as it spins round and round, sinking deeper and deeper into the ripples of the cyclone until he's no longer in sight. And then, the vortex is gone.

What was that?

I look back to find TechnocRat holding his screw, and Dog-Gone's nose pressed against a red button on the cylindrical machine.

"Well, go figure," TechnocRat says, "I guess I didn't need that screw after all."

I'm gonna kill that rat.

"G-Good boy," I mutter to Dog-Gone.

And then everything goes black.

Meta Profile
The Freedom Force
Captain Justice
Class: Super-Strength
Meta:
Ms. Understood
Class: Psychic
Meta:
Glory Girl
Class: Flight
Meta:
Shadow Hawk
Class: None
Meta:
Epic Zero
Class: Meta Manipulator
Meta:
TechnocRat
Class: Super-Intellect
Meta:
Blue Bolt
Class: Super-Speed
Meta:
Master Mime
Class: Magic
Meta:
Makeshift
Class: Energy Manipulator
Meta:

TWO

I SEE DEAD PEOPLE

There's pressure on my stomach. It's hard to breathe.

I open my eyes, and all I see is a black nose.

Then, I'm slobbered to death.

"Get off, Dog-Gone," I say, wiping my cheeks. "You're too heavy. I can't breathe."

Dog-Gone lifts his big paws off my body and I see my parents standing over me, their expressions changing from concern to relief.

"Take it easy, son," Dad says, putting his hand on my arm. "You need to rest."

"Rest?" I say. "Why? And where am I anyway?" I'm lying in some sterile-looking room I've never seen before. Everything is white—the ceiling, the walls, the floor. I try sitting up, but my left arm is hooked into a tube.

What's going on?

"Relax, Elliott," Mom says. "You're back on the Waystation in our new Medi-wing. TechnocRat worked all night to get it finished."

TechnocRat? Hang on, there's something I wanted to say to him. I just can't remember what.

"Elliott, old buddy!" TechnocRat says with unusual gusto. He's standing at the foot of my bed, perched on a steel railing. He looks tired, with droopy whiskers and tiny circles under his eyes. "Boy am I glad to see you so alert. Here's the bad news. You passed out from exhaustion, so we're going to have to shut you down for a while. But there's also good news. We learned you're faster than a T-Rex."

T-Rex? T-Rex!

Without thinking, I pop up and swipe at the rat.

"Elliott!" Dad says, holding me back. "What's gotten into you?"

"Ask him," I huff, slumping back into the bed.

"TechnocRat, what's he talking about?" Mom asks.

"Well," TechnocRat says, running his claws along the railing, "Don't be mad at the kid. He's right. I… messed up. I got so caught up trying to complete my device that he nearly got eaten by a dinosaur. At least the mutt had enough sense to save the day."

Dog-Gone scratches his hindquarters.

"I'm… sorry, Elliott," TechnocRat says, his paws

behind his back. "I guess I can't always expect everything to be perfect. It's a technical flaw of mine."

Wow, TechnocRat apologized. He never ever apologizes—for anything. Part of me still wants to yell at him, but he looks so pathetic I can't.

"Elliott?" Mom says, nodding towards TechnocRat.

I'd love to let him stew a while longer, but I decide to give in, even though I'm still not happy about it.

"Apology accepted," I mutter. "By the way, what did Dog-Gone zap the T-Rex with?"

"Oh, that's my Time Warper device," TechnocRat says. "It's a portable time machine capable of opening a temporary distortion—otherwise known as a wormhole—in the space-time continuum. I invented it years ago but never use it because altering time is risky business. If you travel back into the past and change it in any meaningful way, it could have a ripple effect that significantly compromises the present."

"Influencing events from the past is a major 'no-no' in the superhero rulebook," Dad says. "You should never mess around with time."

"Correct," TechnocRat says, "I didn't want to use the Time Warper, but since dinosaurs are extinct, I figured sending them back to the Jurassic era posed little risk to our current timestream. Fortunately, I was right, but we got lucky. When you're dealing with time you never know, which is why I keep my Time Warper safely tucked away in my lab. But I guess I pulled it out in the nick of time—get it?"

Everyone laughs but me.

"Too soon, huh?" TechnocRat says looking at me nervously. "Well, um, I think I've got an electro photon lightbulb to fix somewhere. I'll check in on you later."

Then, he scampers off the railing and disappears.

"Elliott," Dad says, "You're being way too hard on him. He did the best he could."

"Yeah," I say. "With my life hanging in the balance."

"His methods aren't always conventional," Mom says. "But you know he's a hero through and through."

Suddenly, I feel guilty. I do know he's a hero, that's for sure. Maybe I was too hard on him.

"Sorry," I say. "The whole T-Rex thing was just so intense. Plus, I ran into the Time Trotter and—"

"The Time Trotter?" Dad says. "He was in Keystone City? But he's a Meta 1. He couldn't be responsible for those dinosaurs. He doesn't have that kind of power."

"Well, that's what I thought, too," I say, "It's kind of a long story." I'm about to launch into my whole ordeal with the Time Trotter, his three-eyed friend, and the mysterious Cosmic Key when…

"Alert! Alert! Alert!" the Meta Monitor blares. "Meta 2 disturbance. Repeat: Meta 2 disturbance. Power signature identified as Where-Wolf. Alert! Alert! Alert! Meta 2 disturbance. Power signature identified as Where-Wolf."

"Where-Wolf!" I exclaim, throwing off the covers.

"He's an Energy Manipulator who can teleport all over the place. Not to mention, he's got a terrible dandruff problem. We'd better get—"

"Hold on, hot shot," Dad says, putting a hand on my shoulder. "You're not going anywhere. You need to recover. We'll handle this one with the rest of the team."

"But…," I start.

"But nothing," Mom says, pulling on her Ms. Understood cowl. "Rest up, Elliott. We'll talk more about your 'long story' when we get back. And please, don't go wandering off into trouble this time. Got it?"

"Sheesh," I say. "Fine."

"Dog-Gone," Mom orders, "keep an eye on him. Sit on him if you have to."

Dog-Gone barks in agreement.

"Love you," she calls out as she leaves the room.

"Clearly," I mutter.

Dog-Gone and I stare each other down while the Freedom Flyer disembarks from the Waystation.

We're alone.

Okay, so I didn't get to tell them about the weird three-eyed guy yet, but there's no reason I can't find out more about him myself. I carefully remove the IV from my arm, pull down the covers and step out of bed when my not-so-loyal companion growls in objection.

Seriously?

"Listen," I say, "we're not doing this."

Dog-Gone blocks the door with his big behind.

"Look, when Mom told me not to go wandering off, she didn't mean I couldn't leave my bed. She just meant I shouldn't leave the Waystation."

Dog-Gone growls again, but I really don't have the energy to go into a full negotiation with him.

"Okay, let's cut to the chase. If you move, I'll give you an entire bag of doggie treats and you can get as sick as you want. Does that work for you?"

Dog-Gone's tail starts wagging.

"I thought so. Follow me." We head into the hallway when I realize the Medi-wing is next door to the Galley. Well, that's convenient. I grab a bag of doggie treats from the pantry and pour all the contents into a metal dog dish.

"Knock yourself out," I say, as Dog-Gone starts crunching away. "But if I were you, I'd pace myself. You're cleaning up any invisi-barf."

With Dog-Gone busy gorging himself, I head up to the Monitor Room. If I'm going to find any information about that three-eyed villain, it's going to be here. I hop into the command chair and punch a few buttons on the keypad. The Meta Monitor lights up.

The Meta Monitor is the most extensive database in the world for Metas. If a bad guy used a superpower anywhere, it'll be captured in here. I type in a few search queries: *Red Skin. Three Eyes. Male.*

Then, I wait. I sure wish I grabbed some popcorn. Thirty seconds later, the Meta Monitor spits out:

No Matches Found.

Huh? That's weird. Why isn't the Meta Monitor showing anything? Hang on, it seemed like he was projecting his image from a distance. I add an additional search term: *Alien.*

The Meta Monitor does its thing, and up pops:

No Matches Found.

Well, that's strange. I don't understand how someone could use a Meta power, but not register in the Meta Monitor's database. I try figuring out an explanation, but I can't come up with one. I guess I'll ask Dad when they get back. Maybe he can think of something.

Well, this was a dead end. I set the Meta Monitor back to auto-pilot and slide off the command chair. My legs are crazy sore, so I decide to stretch them out with a long walk.

As I stroll down the hallway, I hear faint footsteps behind me, followed by a low whimper.

"You ate them all, didn't you?" I ask.

Dog-Gone is moving slowly. He looks up and his guilty expression says it all.

"I warned you," I say. "You know, you have absolutely no willpower. I hope you've got a fast metabolism."

We walk in silence for a while, me trying to solve the mystery of the three-eyed man, and Dog-Gone trying not to yack, when we enter a dark corridor.

Suddenly, I get the feeling we're not alone. Like, we're surrounded!

"Who's there—," I start, but as soon as my eyes adjust to the darkness I'm embarrassed. We're surrounded all right, but not because there's a team of bad guys waiting to attack, but because we've wandered into the Hall of Fallen Heroes.

The Hall of Fallen Heroes is a memorial space dedicated to honoring former members of the Freedom Force who gave their lives in the line of duty. Each hero is represented by a life-sized, bronze statue depicting them in full costume.

There are five statues in all.

I flick on the light switch, triggering spotlights that illuminate each one. Honestly, this area of the Waystation creeps me out. When we were younger, Grace and I would play tag all over the Waystation, but we would never come up here. We both agreed it was off limits.

Mom, however, comes up here all the time. She says it gives her perspective whenever she needs to make tough decisions.

There's a giant inscription carved into the wall. It reads: *True Heroes Give So Others May Live.*

I walk down the row of statues.

First up is Rolling Thunder, a Meta 3 Energy Manipulator with the ability to shape and magnify sound. He had a handlebar moustache and wore the insignia of a sound wave stretched across his barrel-shaped chest. Dad said Rolling Thunder was a character and his laugh sounded like a sonic boom.

Next up is Madame Meteorite, a Meta 3 Flyer who wore the symbol of a comet across her bodysuit. She was an astronaut who passed through a strange dust cloud, giving her the ability to defy gravity and glide through any atmosphere, including outer space.

The third statue is of Robot X-treme, a Meta 3 Super-Intellect who was part-man, part-machine. Robot X-treme was a genius with a rare disease that attacked his own body. So, he transferred his brain into a seven-foot tall indestructible robot with built-in weaponry. Dad says Robot X-treme had the most brilliant mind he's ever known, which always sends TechnocRat into a tizzy.

Then there's Dynamo Joe, a Meta 3 Strongman with long hair, a thick beard, and the insignia of a boxing glove on his chest. Dad said Dynamo Joe was not only a former boxing champ, but also a hippie—whatever that means. Dad brags about how he beat Dynamo Joe in an arm-wrestling match. But based on the ridiculous size of Dynamo Joe's biceps, I'm not sure I'm buying it.

Finally, I reach the last statue, which always gives me the chills. That's because it's of a girl about my age. Her name was Sunbolt, and she was a Meta 2 Energy Manipulator with the power to harness solar energy. She wore pigtails, a cape, and had the image of a sun on her top. Mom said she was brave and smart and wanted to learn everything she could to be a great hero.

She was also Dynamo Joe's daughter.

I stare into her determined eyes, and for some

reason, I can't look away. Maybe it's because she was just starting out—sort of like me.

I've never really spent time with the statues before. I guess I can see why Mom comes up here so often. It's a great reminder that playing superhero isn't a game. It's life or death every time you put on the cape.

I mean, these guys sacrificed their lives being heroes.

Could I do that? Would I do that?

"C'mon, Dog-Gone," I say, heading back the way we came. The poor mutt is starting to look green.

Then, I remember all these fallen heroes have something in common.

They were all killed in the battle with Meta-Taker.

The battle that created the Freedom Force.

Thankfully, that monster is out of our lives now.

Well, I'm no closer to solving the mystery of the three-eyed man. I'm wiped, so I head back to my room, drop my utility belt and mask on my desk, and climb into bed. I'm so tired I can't even change out of my costume.

As I lay my head on my pillow, I catch a glimpse of the photograph on my nightstand. It's a picture of my family all together in costume. Of course, Grace's shoulder is blocking half of my face.

Nevertheless, I'm thankful my parents survived that battle with Meta-Taker.

I close my eyes, and as I drift off to sleep, I hear the not-so-sweet sounds of Dog-Gone barfing in my bathroom.

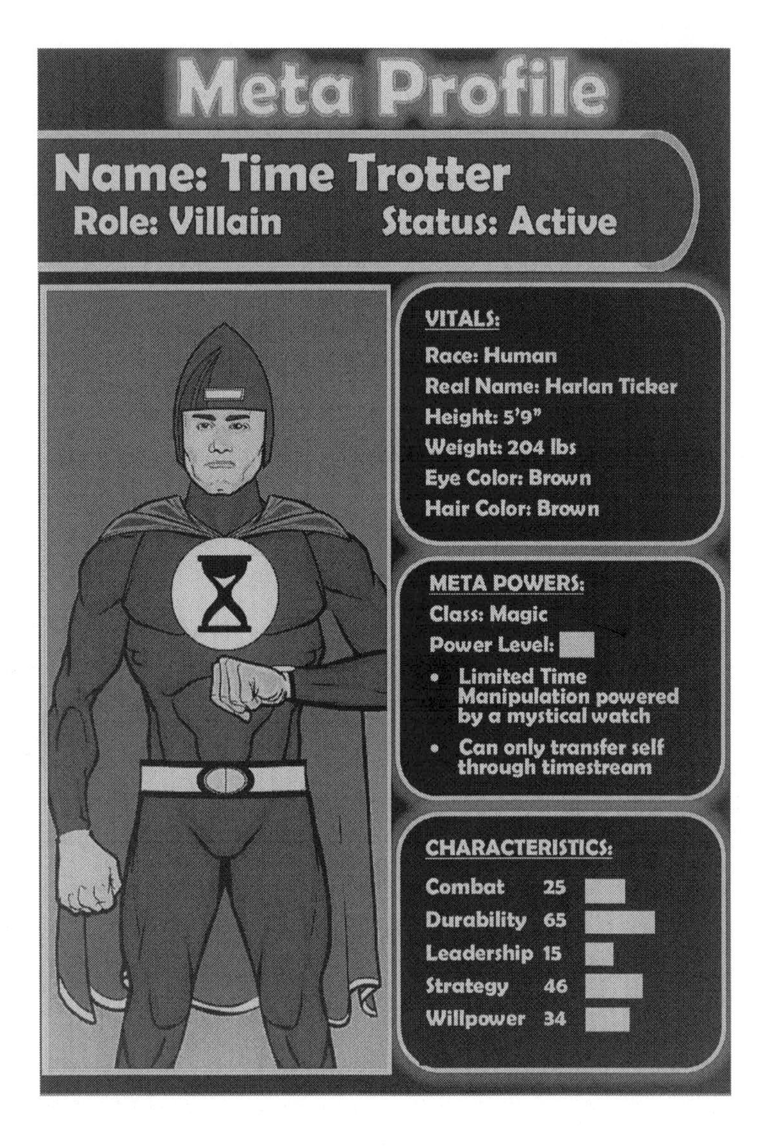
Meta Profile
Name: Time Trotter
Role: Villain
Status: Active
VITALS:
Race: Human
Real Name: Harlan Ticker
Height: 5'9"
Weight: 204 lbs
Eye Color: Brown
Hair Color: Brown
META POWERS:
Class: Magic
Power Level:
• Limited Time Manipulation powered by a mystical watch
• Can only transfer self through timestream
CHARACTERISTICS:
Combat 25
Durability 65
Leadership 15
Strategy 46
Willpower 34

THREE

I FREAK OUT

Have you ever woken up more tired than when you went to sleep? Well, that's how I'm feeling right now.

There's drool running down my chin, and I can't even lift my head off the pillow. I don't know how long I've been out, but based on how heavy my body feels, I'm guessing it's been a while.

Mustering my strength, I roll over and squint at the alarm clock. It reads: *3:23 p.m.* Wow, I've slept in all day! I don't remember ever sleeping this late. I mean, Grace sleeps in all the time, but she's a teenager, that's her job!

My stomach is rumbling, which isn't surprising since I've missed breakfast and lunch. And speaking of food…

"Dog-Gone?" I call out to the bathroom.

The last thing I remember is hearing my poor pooch getting sick. Ugh, I can't imagine what's waiting for me in there. I wish dogs had manners, or at least better aim.

"Dog-Gone?" I call again. "Are you okay?"

I wait for a signal—a bark, a groan, the waving of a white flag. But there's nothing. Since it's so late, I bet Mom let him out of my room so he wouldn't wake me up begging for his breakfast. After all, no matter how bad he's feeling, Dog-Gone never misses a meal.

Then, I notice something weird.

The picture on my nightstand is… different?

Instead of my family, there's a photo of a black cat wearing a blue mask. I have no clue whose cat it is, or how it got there.

I bet Grace is playing a prank on me. After all, I'm always busting on her for streaming hours of mindless cat videos. I bet she snuck in here while I was sleeping and swapped out my picture.

Why are sisters so annoying?

I pull down the covers and throw my legs over the side of the bed. With herculean effort, I trudge over to the bathroom, hoping beyond hope that Dog-Gone didn't leave me too huge of a disaster. But as I peek inside, I'm shocked. The floor is sparkling clean!

Now how's that possible? I swear I heard him barfing up a storm last night. Did Mom or Dad clean it up? Whatever happened, I'm counting my lucky stars.

I catch my reflection in the mirror. My hair looks like

a bird's nest and I'm still wearing my costume. Well, most of my costume anyway. My mask is on my desk and I can't help but notice I'm minus one cape.

Stupid T-Rex.

I think about showering, but my rumbling stomach objects. So, I decide I'll grab a bite first in the Galley. Maybe I'll catch Shadow Hawk making one of his famous peanut butter and banana sandwiches.

I exit my room and pray I run into Dad. No one gets costumes cleaner than Dad. Plus, he's such a stickler for detail I can count on him to sew on a new cape. I just hope he'll do it without his usual lecture on the proper care of Meta gear.

I enter the Galley to find Grace bent over, rummaging through the fridge. I also hear loud munching coming from beneath the dining table, which can only mean one thing—Dog-Gone is back on his furry feet.

"I see you're feeling better, huh?" I say, patting the table-top. "That's great news because you looked so stuffed, I thought you were going to pop."

But instead of a bark, he lets out a high-pitched hiss.

Okay, maybe he's not feeling better.

Grace is still digging around the refrigerator, so I lay a hand on her shoulder and say, "Nice try with that cat picture, but I knew it was—"

Then, she wheels on me, chicken drumstick in hand.

And I realize it's not Grace at all.

Her eyes are red instead of blue. And her hair is

black instead of blond.

"Who-Who are you?" I stammer.

"Funny," she says, her voice deeper than my sister's, "because I was wondering the same thing about you."

Just then, I notice her costume isn't crimson red with white shooting stars. It's all black with a big skull on it!

"You're not Glory Girl," I say.

"Nope," she says. "I'm Gory Girl." Suddenly, a red aura emanates from her hand, and the meat on the chicken drumstick melts away, leaving only the bone!

"Where's the Freedom Force?" I ask.

"The Freedom Force," she scoffs. "We kicked those losers out years ago. Now this place belongs to us—the Freak Force."

The Freak Force?

"Um, I think I woke up on the wrong side of the satellite," I say, backing up to the entrance.

I don't know what's going on, but I can tell that she's sizing me up to be her next chicken drumstick. Time to make my exit. I bang on the dining table. "C'mon, Dog-Gone. Let's go."

But instead of a German Shepherd, out steps a black cat wearing a blue mask. The thing is fluffy and huge, nearly the size of Dog-Gone. Then, I realize it's the same cat as in the picture by my bed!

"Stick him, Scaredy-Cat!" Gory Girl commands.

Scaredy-Cat?

The next thing I know, the cat's claws extend to a

ridiculous size and the feline jumps me! I flail my arms just in time, knocking it back towards Gory Girl. The cat smashes into her, and they both crash into the refrigerator in a tangled mess of hair and paws.

Suddenly, I feel a sharp pain on my right side. I look down to see my costume is ripped from my armpit down to my waist. The cat got me! I've got to get out of here!

I bolt down the hallway.

"Get him!" Gory Girl screams.

What the heck is going on? I'd like to think I'm dreaming, but my side hurts so much I know I'm not.

Something has gone totally bonkers here.

I mean, where's my family? She said the Freak Force kicked the Freedom Force off the Waystation years ago. How is that possible?

I head for the Monitor Room to see if I can find a familiar face, when I hear—

"Don't let him get away!"

That was Gory Girl again! And it sounds like she's rallying her troops! How could I be home, but everyone inside my home is from bizarro world?

And then it hits me. The three-eyed man!

He said he was going back in time.

Did he stop the heroes like he said he was going to do? Did he alter the course of history?

But if that's the case, how am I still here?

I reach the Monitor Room stairwell and I'm about to go up, when I see a pair of boots coming down.

"I'll find him!" comes a voice.

Gotta move!

I book down the hall. If the Freak Force are the only Metas here, then all these guys must be villains.

Just. Freaking. Wonderful.

Well, if that's the case I know one thing, I can't stay here. So, the question becomes, what's the fastest way off a satellite orbiting Earth?

It's useless heading for the Mission Room or the Combat Room because they're both dead ends. I could go for the Hangar to nab a Freedom Flyer or Ferry, but what if they're all gone? Another option is the Transporter Room, but if the timestream *is* screwed up I could be trapped on a world filled with villains or worse.

Then, I get a terrifying thought.

What if going anywhere is useless?

I mean, if my timestream *is* screwed up, the only way to fix it is to go back into the past myself. But how?

I sure wish TechnocRat was here. I know I gave him a hard time, but he'd whip up something in his lab and… and…

That's it!

I've got a plan!

I double back the way I came, running past the Galley and sprinting towards the West Wing. I spot more villains out of the corner of my eye, but I'm not planning on dropping in for a chat. Instead, I huff and puff to my final destination.

TechnocRat's laboratory.

Even though the Freedom Force isn't here anymore, it looks like the lab still is. But the doors are closed and there's yellow cautionary tape on the outside that reads: DANGER. DO NOT ENTER.

Danger? That's weird.

But I'm not going to let some warning tape stop me, because my only escape route is inside that room. At least, I'm hoping it's inside. Of course, if I'm wrong, I've just made the worst decision of my life.

I reach for the keypad, when I notice it's covered in dust. Wait a second, Gory Girl said they kicked the Freedom Force out years ago. So, is it possible no one's been in TechnocRat's lab since then?

I read the warnings on the yellow tape again.

Then, I notice the carpet next to me is singed black.

Suddenly, it clicks!

No one on the Freak Force knows the passcode to TechnocRat's lab. And just like the Vault, TechnocRat boobytrapped the entrance if you input three incorrect codes. Fortunately, I know what the code is.

I'm about to start typing when I hear a high-pitched HISS. I turn to find a black cat sitting in the hallway, licking his paws and watching me through the narrow slits of his blue mask.

What was that superstition about black cats again?

"Listen," I plead. "I'll give you all the doggie—I mean, kitty snacks you want. Just let me go, okay?"

But Scaredy-Cat just keeps on licking, his tail swaying back and forth like a cobra preparing to strike.

I need to up the ante.

"Okay," I say. "How about you let me go, and after I solve this little mix-up, I'll bring you a tasty rat from my timestream. He might be a little bitter going down, but he's totally worth it. Deal?"

But Scaredy-Cat just stands up and arches his back.

What's he doing? Is he going to pounce?

And then, he tilts his head back and lets out the loudest, most ear-piercing MEOW known to cat.

"No deal!" I say, ducking just in time to avoid Scaredy-Cat's sharp-clawed lunge.

I quickly type in the code: C-A-M-E-M-B-E-R-T.

Bingo! The doors swoosh open, splitting the yellow tape in half. I dive through the entrance, seconds before the doors shut closed behind me. I made it!

But when I turn around, my stomach drops.

The lab looks exactly like I remembered it, and that's not a good thing. Beakers, test tubes, and vials line the walls, and the tables are covered with microscopes and machine parts. Clearly, TechnocRat didn't clean-up before he left—not that I expected him to. The guy's a pack rat to the core.

But this is going to be like trying to find a needle in a dozen haystacks. But I can't give up. I've got to find my ticket out of here.

I've got to find the Time Warper device.

I remember TechnocRat saying he kept the Time Warper tucked away in his lab. But where?

I race around, looking under tables, throwing open cabinets, and emptying boxes. Everything is covered in layers of dust, making me sneeze. Clearly, no one's been here in years, but I still haven't found it. I'm pretty sure I know what I'm looking for. I remember it being gray and cylinder-shaped, with a big red button on top.

How hard could this be?

Apparently, a lot harder than I thought.

I'm starting to regret not going for the Hangar.

BOOM!

I jump. They're pounding on the door!

I know it's made of tungsten steel. But I'm not sure how long it can withstand Meta 3 punishment.

I try a few more cabinets, but I can't find the Time Warper anywhere. Then, I have a horrible thought. Why am I even assuming a Time Warper exists in this timestream? Maybe it doesn't. Maybe this was a huge mistake. Boy, wouldn't that be a kick in the pants?

BOOM!

Suddenly, a fist pops through the door.

I'm running out of time! Sweat pours down my forehead as crazy thoughts race through my brain. Maybe I should give myself up? Maybe they'll take it easy on me? Maybe I'm delusional?

Then, I notice a door in the back corner.

Could it be?

I slide across a table, knocking all kinds of doodads to the floor, and yank open the door. It's a closet—a deep closet—filled with giant crates stacked three levels high. I grab the end of one and pull with all my might, but it doesn't open. It's nailed shut! The crates look big enough to hold a Time Warper, but I've got no time to open—

BOOM!

Nope, no time at all!

I'm about to give up when I notice the crates are labeled. Thank goodness someone is organized around here! I read the closest one. It says: *Camembert Cheese.*

Wow, that's a lot of cheese. I scan a few more crates: *Swiss Cheese. Cheddar Cheese. Mozzarella Cheese.*

Ugh! They're all cheese!

This isn't good.

Then, I realize one crate in the back is not like the others. Instead of brown, it's purple. That's peculiar. It's sitting on the top layer, and I can just read part of its label, but not the whole thing. I stretch up on my tippy toes as far as I can go.

All I can make out is: *--arper.*

No! Way!

My heart is racing. These things look too heavy to bring down, so I guess I'll have to go up. But then I realize that even if I make it to the purple crate, I have no way to open it. My eyes dart around the room before landing on a crowbar. Score! I tuck it under my arm and scale the cheese tower.

By the time I reach the top, my arms and legs are shaking. I go into army-crawl mode, moving across the crates until I reach my goal—the purple crate!

I stretch down to read the label. The words are upside down, but it clearly says: *Time Warper.*

Yes!

BOOM! CRASH!

No! They've busted down the door!

"Search the room," Gory Girl says.

There's no time to lose. I take the crowbar, jam it into the purple crate, and push down with all my might. The top pops open and falls to the floor.

CRASH!

Uh-oh.

"What's that?" Gory Girl asks.

I dig inside the crate and pull out a cylindrical device.

Yes!

My hands are shaking as I hold it. There's a yellow label on the side that reads: *Warning: This is a portable Time Machine. Before operating, please ensure all parts are securely…*

Yada, yada, yada. I don't have time for this!

I set it on top of a neighboring crate and point it at me. Then, I notice there's a keypad and a counter on the side. The keypad reads: *WHERE*, and the counter reads: *WHEN.*

Where and when? Two very excellent questions.

What should I enter?

Just then, I notice something strange.

Taped to the red button is a small, handwritten note that says: *For Elliott.*

For … me? What the…?

I unfold the paper, it's crinkly and yellowed at the edges, like it's been here a long time.

It reads: *WHERE: Keystone City, WHEN: -30 years, 3 months, 10 days.*

That's weird? I scratch my head, when it dawns on me that someone is telling me where to go!

But who?

Unfortunately, I'll have to figure that out later.

I shove the note into my pocket and type K-E-Y-S-T-O-N-E-C-I-T-Y into the keypad and set the counter to -30 years, 3 months, and 10 days.

Then, I hear a HISS.

I turn to find Scaredy-Cat's face peering over the top crate! They found me!

It's time travel time!

I punch the red button.

"Hey!" Gory Girl yells. "Stop right—!"

But I never hear the end of her sentence, because I'm spiraling into a wave of green energy.

And then I'm gone.

Meta Profile
The Freak Force
Gory Girl
Class: Energy Manipulator
Meta:
Scaredy-Cat
Class: Meta-morph
Meta:

FOUR

I GET GROOVY

I think I'm gonna hurl.

I've never been a big fan of amusement parks, and my Time Warper experience was like a teacup ride on steroids. In fact, it kind of felt like I was being sucked through a million bathtub drains. But finally, after what seemed like an eternity, I crashed to the ground.

I've got no clue where I am, but at least I managed to escape the Freak Force—so hooray for that. Now for the big question. Did the Time Warper actually deliver me to the right place?

Well, I seem to be sitting between two buildings and staring at a bunch of garbage cans. So, I'd say I've landed in an alley. But how do I know it's the right alley? Then, I notice a crumpled newspaper in the corner. I crawl a few feet over and pick it up. Gross, it's totally soggy and nearly disintegrates in my hands, but I recognize it as the Keystone City Gazette. So, I'm in the right place.

Then, I pull out my scrunched-up note and re-read it: *-30 years, 3 months, and 10 days.* Wow! This seems to match the date on the newspaper. But I need to know for sure.

Even though I'm still feeling dizzy, I get to my feet and step onto the sidewalk when I hear something loud approaching. I dive back just as a van motors past. It looks like one of those old-fashioned VW vans—with a white top, blue body, and whitewall tires. It even has a peace symbol on its side.

But then I realize something. That van wasn't old-fashioned. In fact, it's just right for the time period I'm standing in. I peer around the corner and my eyes bulge.

This is Keystone City alright, but it's the Keystone City of the past. Everything is different, from the cars to the street lamps to the buildings. Other than the bakery and the bank, I don't recognize any of the other shops, like the Keystone City Record Store which is offering two-for-one vinyl deals on Mondays.

What the heck is vinyl anyway?

Just then, a group of teenagers walks past and I pull back. The girls are wearing plaid pants, colorful sweaters, and headbands in their hair. The guys are wearing turtlenecks, striped sweaters, and polyester pants. Okay, no kid from my school would be caught dead dressed like this.

So, that seals it—I made it!

Inside I do a happy dance. The Time Warper worked! I mean, what are the odds of that? Now all I need to do is find the Freedom Force, fix my timestream problem, and jump back home, which hopefully will have returned to normal.

This should be a piece of cake!

I'm about to set foot into the street again, when I suddenly hear TechnocRat's voice in my brain: *If you travel back into the past and change it in any meaningful way, it could have a ripple effect that significantly compromises the present.*

I stop myself. What am I thinking? I can't go wandering around Keystone City like this! I'm still in costume!

This is bad news. I mean, I'm a kid from the future! If anyone sees me, it could cause a chain reaction that screws up everything! I've got to get some normal clothes so I can explore the city without attracting attention. But how?

Then, I spot a miracle.

Directly across the street is a clothing store! I read the awning. It says: *Groovy Threads Clothing Store.* Bingo!

Except I've got one problem. I don't have any money. Usually, I keep twenty bucks in my utility belt, but I left it in my room. Genius move.

So, how can I pay for new clothes? All I have to offer is child labor. Maybe if I beg hard enough, they'll let me sweep the floor?

But first things first. I need to get across the street without being seen. I look around, but there aren't any blankets or towels to cover me up. In fact, I can't even find a freaking cardboard box!

So, there's one option left. I position myself at the edge of the alley and wait for traffic to die down. What I wouldn't give right now for Blue Bolt's speed or Dog-Gone's invisibility.

It takes forever, but when my moment comes, I hustle across the street and bound through the front door of Groovy Threads. As soon as I enter, a bell RINGS announcing my arrival. So much for stealth mode.

Fortunately, the store is empty.

There's music in the background. It sounds like that old disco music mom plays on the Waystation. She tries to get me to dance with her, but I never give in.

Well, sometimes I don't.

Anyway, I scan the merchandise until I find the boys section. They have a wide selection of shirts and pants, but they're nothing like I'm used to. The shirts are all flowery-patterned button downs with huge collars, and the pants are super slim with bell bottoms.

Seriously? People actually wore this stuff?

"Hey, dude," comes a voice from behind me.

I nearly jump out of my skin. I turn around to find a big man with green eyes, long brown hair, and a beard staring at me. His arms are so big they look like they're about to burst out of his shirt. Where'd he come from?

"What's your bag, man?" he asks.

My bag? What's he's talking about?

"I mean, what can I help you with today?" he asks.

"Oh," I say. "I was hoping to try some things on."

"We don't sell Halloween outfits here," he says.

Halloween outfits? What's he talking about? Then, I realize he's referring to my superhero costume.

"Oh, yeah," I say. "Good one. No, I was looking for regular clothes."

"Groovy," he says, looking me up and down. "Are you from Keystone City?"

"Y—," I start, but then change direction. "I mean, no. I'm from out of town. Just passing through."

"Oh, okay," he says, nodding. But he looks at me suspiciously. "No problem. What do you need?"

"Um, a shirt," I say. "And some pants. And socks. And a belt. And—"

"Got it," he says, stopping me. "I'll hook you up. Why don't you chill out in the fitting room?"

He guides me into a small room behind a beaded curtain. I sit down on a stool and look at my reflection in the mirror. I look like such a mess I'm surprised the guy let me stay in his store.

"Here," he says moments later, pushing a stack of clothes through the curtain. "Try these on."

"Thanks," I say. I put on underwear, black socks, a blue-and-white plaid shirt, brown bell bottom pants, and a pair of red-and-white Converse sneakers. Strangely, I've never been so excited to see underwear.

"So, where are you from?" he asks.

Oh, jeez! If I say I'm from some place he knows, he might start asking me detailed questions. Better to stay vague. "Um, here and there. My parents move a lot."

Please, please, stop asking questions.

"I see," he says. "Do the clothes fit?"

"Yes, thanks," I say, checking myself in the mirror. Surprisingly, everything fits perfectly. I roll up my superhero costume and tuck it under my arm. Now comes the hard part. How am I going to pay for this?

"Um," I say, stepping out of the fitting room. "Sorry, but I just realized I don't have any money. Maybe I can sweep the floor for you? I'm happy to stay all night."

I brace myself for the worst.

But the man just smiles and says, "Nah, it's on me."

"What?" I say. "Are you serious?"

"Sure," the man says. "Styles change fast around here, and that outfit will get more use on you than on one of my mannequins. Just do me a solid and if anyone asks you where you got your look, tell them you came to Groovy Threads. Deal?"

"Sure," I say, stunned. "Thanks."

"Would you like a bag for your costume," he says pointing to my Epic Zero outfit under my arm. "I mean, your Halloween outfit, of course."

"Um, sure," I say.

The man goes behind the counter and brings out a plastic bag with the Groovy Threads logo on the side.

"Here you go," he says. "Be careful out there."

"Gee, thanks," I say.

"No sweat," he says with a wink. "See you around."

I step out of the store still in shock. Well, that was lucky. Weird, but lucky. At least I look normal enough to blend into the crowd. Now to find the Freedom Force.

Just then, I see a dog walking on the opposite side of the street. It's a German Shephard, just like Dog-Gone, but its fur is gray and black instead of brown and black. Boy, I really miss my partner-in-crime.

Suddenly, my eyes get all watery and it hits me. If I don't solve this time-travelling mess, I may never see him again. I rub my eyes and look for that dog again.

He's stopped at the bakery in front of a basket of baguettes. He's not wearing a collar, and his owner doesn't seem to be around. The poor fella must be lost. I can only imagine the heartache he's going through. He's probably tired and hungry, just like me. I wish I had some doggie treats to give him.

But then, all of my sympathy goes out the window as the pooch looks left, then right, then disappears into thin air! I blink hard. Are my eyes playing tricks on me?

The next thing I know, a baguette is magically lifted out of its basket, and takes off down the street!

No! Freaking! Way!

He can turn invisible! And he stole the bread!

I take off after him. He's really fast, which isn't surprising since he has a two-leg advantage. My mind, however, is racing faster than my body.

First of all, that can't be Dog-Gone. He's the wrong color. Besides, I'm, like, thirty years in the past.

"Stop!" I yell.

Without breaking stride, I see the bread point towards me, then go even faster. He knows I'm chasing him! Okay, calling out to him was a huge mistake.

As we pass by, strangers point at us and I realize how absolutely nuts this must look. I mean, it's not every day you see a goofily-dressed kid in hot pursuit of a runaway baguette. But I need to stop that mutt no matter what. After all, he's a Meta, which means he's my best shot at finding other Metas—like my family!

But the dog has the advantage and he knows it. He's staying low, cutting around people, bicycles, and park benches. I'm doing my best to keep up, but I'm losing ground every second. Then, he flies across the street, barely avoiding an oncoming car.

I stop at the crosswalk, look both ways, and pick up the trail. He's way ahead now. If I don't do something, he'll get away for good.

I hop up on a bench, concentrate hard, and cast my negation powers far and wide. If I can negate his powers, I can remove his invisibility. But I don't see him anywhere. He's gone.

Well, it was probably pointless anyway. Even if I

could see him, I couldn't do anything to stop his natural speed. So, there goes my only hope. Now what?

I step off the bench when—

CRASH!

Shards of glass come flying at me. The next thing I know, two guys in all black leap through a busted storefront window. They're wearing stockings over their heads and carrying big sacks over their shoulders. I look up at the sign on the building. It reads: *Keystone City Jewelers.*

It's a robbery! And it's happening right in front of me! My first instinct is to stop these guys, but then I remember I'm not supposed to do anything. The last thing I want is to cause a time cataclysm.

Suddenly, I hear SIRENS.

Great. The boys in blue will handle this.

The crooks pull out guns as a fleet of police cars screech into view, blocking all escape routes. Car doors fly open everywhere, and the next thing I know, there's dozens of pistols pointed our way.

"Drop your weapons!" shouts an officer through a megaphone. "You're surrounded!"

"What now, Weasel?" the bigger goon asks.

I want to say, 'now you get arrested, numbskull,' but apparently, 'Weasel' has other ideas.

"Easy, Moose," Weasel says. "It's time for Plan B."

Plan B? I wonder what these morons came up with for Plan B? Then, I realize they're looking at me!

"Grab the kid!" Weasel orders.

Uh-oh.

Before I can move, Moose grabs me and puts me in a headlock. Then, Weasel presses his gun to my temple! I try pulling free, but I can't. And to top it off, my Meta powers are useless against these guys. They're Zeroes!

Somehow, by trying not to interfere, I've put myself in the worst situation possible. I'm a hostage!

Just. Freaking. Wonderful.

"Release the child," the officer demands.

Did he call me a child? Seriously?

"Get lost cop and maybe we'll think about it!" Weasel shouts back, pulling back the gun's hammer.

Then I get a weird thought. Can I die in the past?

"Stand back, officers!" booms a male voice. "I've got this situation under control!"

Just then, a masked figure lands ten feet in front of us. He's wearing a red, white, and blue costume with a giant American flag across his chest. He has long blond hair, blue eyes, and a square jaw. At first, I'm elated that I'm about to be saved. But as I take a closer look, I realize he looks like he just graduated from high school.

"Liberty Lad!" Moose yells. "Get lost!"

Liberty Lad? I've never heard of…

"Sorry," Liberty Lad says. "But it's Fight Time!"

Fight Time. Fight Time? Hold on, there's only one Meta I know who says that. I study Liberty Lad's face more closely and my jaw drops.

O.M.G!

It's… Dad? But way younger!

"Back off," Weasel orders. "Or we'll waste the kid."

"Let's talk this over," Liberty Lad suggests, sounding surprisingly nervous. "Don't make any rash decisions."

"Step aside!" comes a female voice. "And let a real hero handle this!"

Suddenly, a masked girl appears. She's wearing a red bodysuit with a lightning bolt on the front. She has a brown ponytail and brown eyes. She looks as young as Dad, but I'd know that voice anywhere.

It's Mom!

So, that can only mean one thing.

The three-eyed man failed!

The Freedom Force is still together!

"I *am* a real hero," Liberty Lad says, clearly annoyed. "And I don't need your help. So why don't you take your mind tricks somewhere else, Brainstorm."

Brainstorm? I didn't know she called herself that.

"Really?" she says mockingly. "Then tell me, why is the innocent hostage here still a hostage?"

"Because I was just about to act," he says. "Until I was assaulted by your rudeness."

Hang on a second, are they… arguing?

"Rudeness?" she says. "You're one to call me—"

But as they bicker back and forth, it dawns on me.

My parents aren't together at all.

In fact, they hate each other.

Meta Profile

Name: Liberty Lad

Role: Hero **Status: Inactive**

- **Currently operating as Captain Justice**

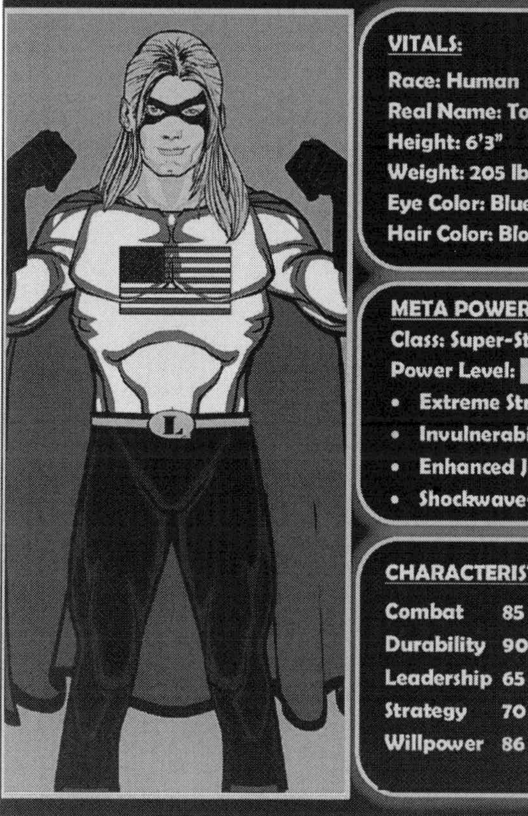

VITALS:

Race: Human
Real Name: Tom Harkness
Height: 6'3"
Weight: 205 lbs
Eye Color: Blue
Hair Color: Blonde

META POWERS:

Class: Super-Strength
Power Level:

- Extreme Strength
- Invulnerability
- Enhanced Jumping
- Shockwave-Clap

CHARACTERISTICS:

Combat	85
Durability	90
Leadership	65
Strategy	70
Willpower	86

FIVE

I MUST BE DREAMING

I can't believe what's happening.

I mean, I'm not even supposed to be here. The only reason I traveled into the past is to fix my present, which somehow went completely bonkers! And I suspect it has everything to do with that mysterious three-eyed man and his plan to find that Cosmic Key he was mumbling about.

But that's not even my biggest problem right now. Both Dad and TechnocRat told me the number one rule for time travel is never to interfere in any way. Yet, here I am, being held at gunpoint by a couple of petty criminals.

So, I pretty much flunked that one.

But then, just as I'm desperately searching for the Freedom Force for help, my parents show up out of the blue as barely adults with completely embarrassing superhero names. You'd think my job was done, except they're way too busy arguing with each other to bother saving me.

You know, their kid from the future.

I've got a headache.

"Sorry, Brainstorm," Dad says. "But I work solo. That means alone."

"Gee, thanks for the vocabulary lesson, Captain Grammar," Mom scoffs, "but I know perfectly well what 'solo' means. In fact, it's how I prefer operating as well."

"Well, feel free to leave," Dad says. "Because I don't team-up with Metas I can't trust. Not with everything that's been going on."

Wait, what's he talking about? What's going on?

"My thoughts exactly," Mom says. "So, let's just say I'm keeping an eye on you."

"Me?" Dad says. "You think I'm responsible?"

Oh, jeez. Here they go again.

"Weasel," Moose whispers. "Let's get out of here."

"Yeah," Weasel says. "Follow my lead."

The two morons tiptoe backward, taking me with them! And my parents are completely oblivious!

"—not infringe on my territory," Dad says.

"This isn't your territory," Mom says. "I don't see the words 'Inflated Ego" on any street sign anyw—"

"Hey!" I interject. "Sorry to bug you in the middle of this enlightening conversation, but are either of you 'superheroes' actually planning on doing anything super?

You know, like helping me out?"

"Shut it, kid," Weasel says, digging the tip of his gun into my temple. "You heroes back off! And that goes for you cops, too! Drop your weapons or the kid gets it!"

My parents look my way, their jaws hanging open. They were so caught up arguing, they forgot we were even here. And the cops can't do anything but lower their pistols. So, this is pretty much going from bad to worse.

"See, Moose," Weasel says, puffing out his chest. "I told you I had a—yeooow!"

Suddenly, I feel an intense burst of heat, and Weasel grabs his right foot like it's on fire.

"Ahh!" he screams, hopping around before falling to the ground, his gun rattling on the pavement.

"Weasel?" Moose says, letting go of me.

I drop hard to my hands and knees.

"What happened?" Moose cries, but as soon as he raises his gun, the barrel melts into a gloppy mess.

"Sorry," comes a female voice, "but I guess that's too hot to handle."

The next thing I know, a girl with red pigtails and a yellow cape blazes out of the sky and lands with her back to me. Moose swings at her but misses badly. The girl socks him in the gut and then kicks him square in the jaw, sending several of his teeth flying. Moose topples over and doesn't get back up.

"M-Make it stop!" Weasel begs, his foot smoking.

"Not a fan of a hot foot, huh?" the girl says. She

waves her hand, and the smoke subsides.

"T-Thank you," he says, relief washing over his face.

Just then, the police come charging in. They slap handcuffs on the crooks and yank the stockings off their ugly mugs.

"Well, I think the good guys have this one under control," the girl says.

Then, she turns to face me, and I do a double take.

She's around my age, with bright green eyes and a big smile. For some reason, I feel like I've seen her before, but I can't place her. And then my eyes land on the yellow sun insignia on her costume.

O. M. G.

It's … It's …

"Sunbolt," Mom says.

Sunbolt? B-But, she's… she's…

"In the flesh," Sunbolt says. "Sorry to barge in like that, but it looked like the kid needed some help."

"You did the right thing," Dad says, then he walks over to me and reaches out. "Sorry about that, kid. Can I help you up?"

I reach for his hand, but then stop myself.

What am I doing? I mean, how can I ask them for help without revealing who I am? It's not like I can just say: 'Hi there, I'm Elliott, your son from the far-flung future.' That could affect the past in such a dramatic way it could change everything! I need to think this through.

"Are you okay, kid?" Dad asks.

"Um, yeah," I say. "I'm fine." I clasp his hand and he pulls me to my feet, but I keep my head down. The last thing I want to make eye contact. I can't let him get a good look at my face.

Then, Mom comes over.

"I'm so sorry," she says, putting her hand on my shoulder. "I guess we got so distracted we forgot what we're here to do. But I have to say, you were really brave back there. I'm impressed."

"Oh, thanks," I say. I've got to stay low key. The worst thing that could happen right now is for Mom to read my mind. "Anyway, I guess I'll be going now."

"You dropped your stuff," Dad says, leaning over.

My heart skips a beat.

My Groovy Threads bag is on the ground—and my Epic Zero costume is sticking halfway out of the bag!

"No!" I yell.

Dad stops in his tracks.

"Sorry," I say more evenly. "Thanks, but I'll get it." I scoop up the bag and shove the costume back inside. "It's just a silly Halloween costume."

"Well, thanks again, Sunbolt," Mom says. "It's nice to know there are some heroes you can still trust."

"Now what's that supposed to mean?" Dad asks.

"You're a smart guy," Mom says. "I'm sure you'll figure it out. Later, Sunbolt. Glad you're okay, kid."

Then, she runs off.

"Well," Dad says, "she's got some nerve. See you

around, Sunbolt. And be careful out there. These days you can't be too sure which Meta's are on your side."

Dad departs and Sunbolt and I are all alone.

"Are you okay?" Sunbolt asks. "You look like you've seen a ghost."

Well, how am I supposed to look? I mean, the last time I saw Sunbolt was in the Hall of Fallen Heroes. And that was her memorial bronze statue!

Yet, here she stands, completely alive and breathing. I feel totally awkward talking to her. After all, I know she died in the battle with Meta-Taker. But it's not like I can tell her that.

"Hey, it's okay," she continues. "I can imagine this was overwhelming for you. Most people never come face-to-face with Metas."

Oh, if she only knew.

"Um, yeah," I say, smoothing out my wrinkled shirt. "You're probably right. Thanks for saving me."

"No problem," she says. "That's what heroes are for. Do you need a lift home? I can fly you there."

Home?

For some reason, the word hits me hard. Believe me, I'd love nothing more than to go home. Except my home is in another time and place. Here, my parents don't even know I exist. And apparently, they'd be fine if the other one didn't exist either.

Suddenly, I feel kind of … lost.

"What's wrong?" she asks.

Ugh, I'm tearing up. This is so embarrassing!

"Nothing," I say, wiping my face. "I'm good."

"What's your name?" she asks.

"El—," I start, but then stop myself. Am I nuts? I can't tell her my real name! "I'm… Eric."

"Are you homeless, Eric?" she asks. "Is that why you're so upset?"

Great question. Now how am I supposed to answer that one? "Yeah," I say. "I guess."

"I'm so sorry," she says. "Look, you're probably hungry. Why don't you come with me for a bit? I've got some friends that can help you out."

Well, I know I can't do that. I mean, I'm supposed to be laying low while I'm here. But as soon as she said the word 'hungry,' my stomach rumbled. I never did get food back on the Waystation and it feels like I haven't eaten in days, which may actually be the case.

"What do you think?" she asks. "It's good stuff."

My head says 'no,' but my stomach rumbles 'yes.' I wonder if Dog-Gone makes his decisions this way?

"Sure," I say, shocking myself. "Thanks."

"Great," she says. "But first, I'll need to blindfold you."

"What?" I say

"Trust me," she says. "It's safer for you that way."

Safer? Then, I realize if she wants to blindfold me, she must be taking me somewhere secret—like to her headquarters where I can find other Metas.

"Okay," I say. "Let's do it."

"Great," she says. "I just need a blindfold." She scans the ground and picks up one of the goon's discarded body stockings. "This should do it."

She doubles the stocking and covers my eyes, tying it tight behind my head. I can't see a thing.

"How's that?" she asks.

"Surprisingly effective," I say.

"Great," she says.

Then, she wraps her arms around me and takes off. But as my feet leave the ground, I get a funny feeling in my stomach, and I know it's not air sickness.

I mean, I feel so totally out of place here. I may be in Keystone City, but it's not my Keystone City. And the way Mom and Dad were arguing made it seem like something strange is going on in the Meta community.

"Sunbolt," I call out, "can I ask you something?"

"Sure, Eric," she answers. "What is it?"

Eric? Why'd she call me… oh yeah.

"Why did D—, I mean Liberty Lad, say that these days you can't be sure which Metas are on your side?"

"Well," she says, "some Meta's have gone missing. But it's nothing to worry about. I'm sure they're fine."

"Oh, okay," I say casually, but my alarm bells go off.

Metas are missing? That's not good.

I wonder if it's related to why I'm here. But before I can give it serious thought—

"We've arrived," Sunbolt says.

My feet touch down gently.

"Wait here," she says.

I hear latches unlocking and then a door screeches open. Sunbolt takes my hand and leads me inside.

Music fills my ears. It's disco music, just like what was playing when I entered Groovy Threads. Man, I guess this stuff was hot back then.

Then, she stops me, and the door slams shut behind us, cutting off the music. I hear latches being relocked.

"Okay, Eric," Sunbolt says, "meet my friends."

As my blindfold comes off, I see three people seated at a table in front of us—two men and one woman.

And they're wearing costumes!

But why do they look so familiar?

[Greetings, tiny Meta Zero unit,] comes an automated voice, startling me from behind.

But as I turn around, I take a step back.

A giant robot is staring down at me.

Wait, I've seen him before!

Then, I look back at the people.

Hang on.

I-I know these guys!

They're the other dead members of the Freedom Force!

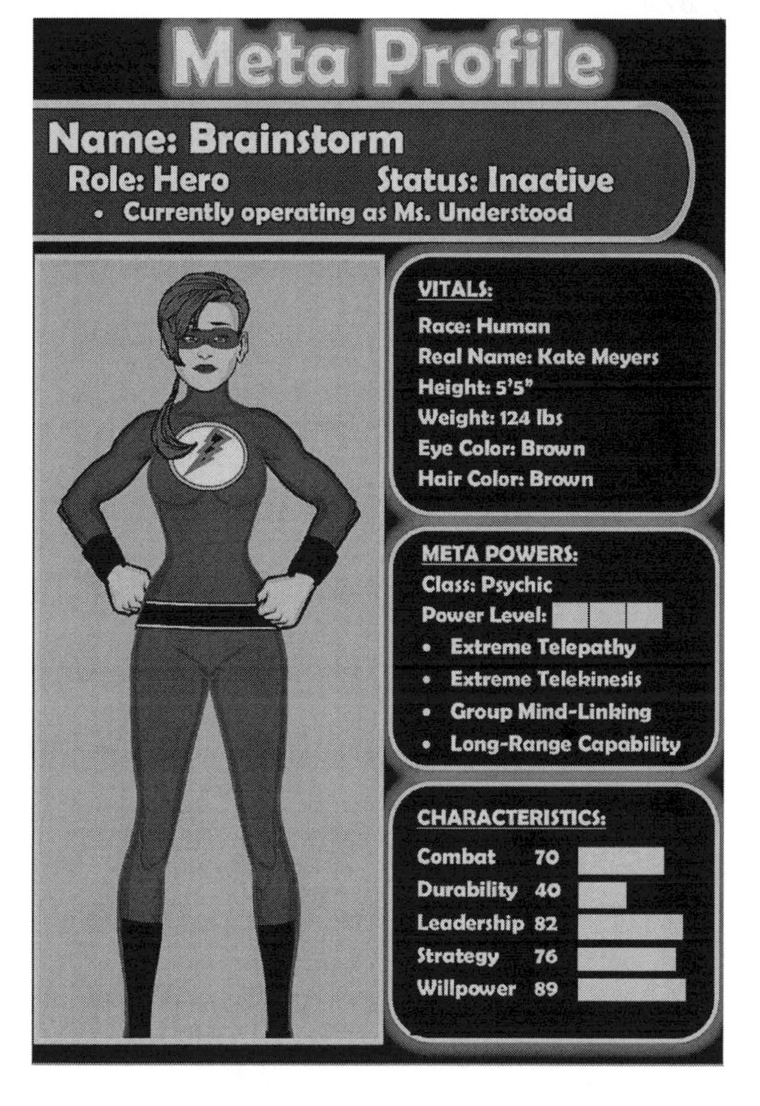
Meta Profile
Name: Brainstorm
Role: Hero
Status: Inactive
• Currently operating as Ms. Understood
VITALS:
Race: Human
Real Name: Kate Meyers
Height: 5'5"
Weight: 124 lbs
Eye Color: Brown
Hair Color: Brown
META POWERS:
Class: Psychic
Power Level:
• Extreme Telepathy
• Extreme Telekinesis
• Group Mind-Linking
• Long-Range Capability
CHARACTERISTICS:
Combat 70
Durability 40
Leadership 82
Strategy 76
Willpower 89

SIX

I CAN'T BELIEVE MY EYES

I'm in shock.

I mean, I'm standing in front of a room full of heroes who are supposed to be dead! But because I've traveled into the past, they're all still alive!

"Come in," says a large, masked man with a handlebar mustache. He's wearing a green costume with the image of a sound wave across his chest. "Any friend of Sunbolt's is a friend of mine. I'm Rolling Thunder."

I want to blurt out: 'Yeah, I know exactly who you are because I just visited your memorial in the Hall of Fallen Heroes.' But I manage to keep my mouth shut. No need to open that can of worms.

"Please sit down," says the woman, who pulls out a chair. She's wearing a red costume with a comet blazing across her top. "I'm Madame Meteorite, and I'm guessing you could use something to eat."

"I'll fix him something," says the second masked man. He has long brown hair, a beard, and is wearing a purple costume with a red boxing glove on his chest. I already know who he is, but he introduces himself anyway. "I'm Dynamo Joe," he says. "Please, come in. Don't be shy. And don't let that bucket-of-bolts scare you. He gets cranky when he hasn't had his tune-up."

[I am not cranky,] the robot says. [I am Robot X-treme.]

I look the metal monolith up and down. He certainly looks intimidating, with his massive robotic hands and rocket-powered legs. And then I remember that inside this tin can is an actual human brain.

"Go ahead, Eric," Sunbolt says. "Sit down."

I'd love to, but I hesitate. After seeing these guys, I feel like I've made a big mistake coming here. But I'm also in way too deep to back out now. Plus, I'm starving. So, I guess I should just eat something and try not to screw anything up—like the entire future, for instance.

"Um, thanks," I say, sitting down. I pull up to the circular table and take in my surroundings. Dozens of monitors line the walls, projecting images of famous landmarks: like the White House, the Statue of Liberty, and the Grand Canyon. Giant computer consoles occupy every corner, studded with buttons, radio dials, and flashing lights. A dizzying number of cables crisscross the ceiling, all connecting into a centralized power source.

"We call this the Nerve Center," Sunbolt says, taking the seat next to me. "It's where we monitor the globe for trouble. Robot X-treme designed the whole thing. It's super advanced."

"Oh, I can tell," I say. I'd love to tell them about the Monitor Room TechnocRat designed, but I can't. That would blow my cover. But maybe if I play dumb, I can collect some information. "So, where are we anyway?"

"Nice try," Sunbolt says, "But we can't tell you that. Remember the blindfold? It's safer for you if the location of our headquarters remains a secret."

"Right," I say. Well, that didn't work.

"Here you go," Dynamo Joe says, placing a plate of fried chicken, corn, and steamed broccoli in front of me.

The smell hits my nostrils and I salivate.

"We hope you like it," Rolling Thunder says.

But I can't respond, because I'm stuffing my face.

"I'll take that as a yes," Rolling Thunder says.

"Mmmhmm," I mumble, gobbling a drumstick. Man, I didn't realize I was this hungry. I probably look like Dog-Gone when we found him inhaling our holiday ham.

"Glad you like it," Madame Meteorite says, "Rolling Thunder made it. He's quite the chef."

"It's a hobby," Rolling Thunder says.

After I polish off my plate, I lean back in my chair, totally stuffed. Okay, I ate that way too fast.

"Well, if he were a Meta, I know what his power

would be," Rolling Thunder says.

"Chill, Thunder," Dynamo Joe says, reaching for my plate. "Glad you digged it. Would you like more, Eric?"

I look around for Eric, when I remember, that's me!

"Oh, no!" I say quickly. "That was great, thanks." But as he takes my plate away, I stare into his green eyes and get a strange feeling that I've seen him before.

"Groovy Threads?" Dynamo Joe asks, admiring my bag. "That's a happening place, isn't it?"

Then it hits me!

He's the guy from Groovy Threads!

"Yeah," I say. "Very happening."

"So," Madame Meteorite says to Sunbolt. "How'd you two meet?"

"Well," Sunbolt says, "I rescued him from a hostage situation. Liberty Lad and Brainstorm were both there, but they couldn't get the job done."

"Good work," Dynamo Joe says. "And I'm glad Eric is okay, but you have to be careful around other Metas. We talked about this."

"Da--," Sunbolt starts, but then stops herself. "I mean, Dynamo Joe, the bad guys had him at gunpoint! What should I have done? Let the kid croak?"

"Of course not," Dynamo Joe says. "But some heroes aren't who they claim to be. And that's dangerous."

Dangerous? Wait a second, is he calling Mom and Dad dangerous?

"I had it under control," Sunbolt says.

"I'm sure Blue Bolt and Master Mime thought the same thing, but now they're missing," Dynamo Joe says.

Blue Bolt and Master Mime are missing?

The room is silent. I can feel the tension.

"Um, sorry to interrupt," I say, "but what exactly happened to Blue Bolt and Master Mime?"

"We think they were ambushed," Rolling Thunder says. "Word on the street is that they were on a mission with some other 'hero' who probably betrayed them. Who knows? It could have been Liberty Lad or Brainstorm."

What?

"Hang on," I say. "Everyone knows that Liberty Lad and Brainstorm are heroes."

"Are they?" Rolling Thunder says. "Or is one of them the Trickster?"

"The Trickster?" I say. "Who's that?"

"That's what the hero community is calling the traitor," Madame Meteorite says, flashing an annoyed look at Rolling Thunder. "But don't worry about it. Some people just like being dramatic around here."

"Am I being dramatic?" Rolling Thunder asks. "Or a realist?"

"Anyway," Dynamo Joe interrupts, "everyone should just remember that all of the people we trust are right here in this room. We're the real heroes."

"But so are Liberty Lad and Brainstorm," I blurt out.

"They're real heroes too. I mean, they're part of the Freedom Force."

"The Freedom Force?" Rolling Thunder says. "What's the Freedom Force?"

Whoops! Clearly, the Freedom Force doesn't even exist yet. Now I've really stepped in it.

"Power Alert!" screams an alarm, accompanied by flashing lights.

What's that?

"Power Alert!" it repeats. "Power Alert! Meta Powers Detected!"

The heroes jump up and congregate in front of a squat, round computer. The monitor screen looks like one of those old-time radar screens. Every time the pulsar sweeps over the United States, it flashes. This must be their version of a Meta Monitor!

"Who is it?" Sunbolt asks.

"Not sure," Dynamo Joe says, punching a few keys, "but there's a lot of them."

The image changes to video and we're looking at Mount Rushmore. It's the national monument where sixty-foot high faces of former presidents are carved out of granite. I've never been there, but it looks pretty cool.

Suddenly, a strange creature blocks the camera. Whatever it is, it's absolutely ginormous, with huge wings and a long, pointy beak. We watch as it circles the mountain and then comes back around into view.

My eyes go wide.

I-I can't believe it.

It's a… a…

"Pterodactyl?" Madame Meteorite says.

The creature flies straight towards the camera and then veers off at the last second.

Then, it's joined by another. And then another.

But that can only mean…

"How did those things get here?" Madame Meteorite asks. "They must be millions of years old."

[You are correct, flying Meta 3 unit,] Robot X-treme says. [Based on scientific evidence, Pterodactylus antiquus lived approximately 201.3 million years ago. Therefore, we can conclude with one hundred percent certainty they must have traveled through the timestream.]

"The timestream?" Rolling Thunder says, scratching his head. "So, these dingbats traveled through time?"

[Yes, mustached Meta 3 unit,] Robot X-treme says. [A Meta disturbance caused a ripple in the timestream, triggering the Nerve Center's alarm.]

"But how did that happen?" Sunbolt asks.

I want to tell them all about the Time Trotter and what happened in my time, but I know I can't. I mean, I've gone way too far just by being here. But then—

"Power Alert!" the monitor blares again. "Power Alert! Meta Powers Detected!"

"What now?" Sunbolt says.

"More prehistoric problems," Dynamo Joe says, typing into the keyboard. "Right here in Keystone City."

Then, up pops an image that gives me the chills.

It's a T-Rex. My least favorite dinosaur.

"It's in the woods," Dynamo Joe says. "Near the ArmaTech Laboratories building."

ArmaTech? I know ArmaTech. That's a weapons lab. And it's also where TechnocRat was injected with some secret brain serum that turned him into the world's smartest creature.

"Isn't that a private company run by some rich, mad scientist?" Madame Meteorite asks.

"That's the one," Rolling Thunder says. "The mad scientist's name is Norman Fairchild. He's a billionaire who develops dangerous weapons and sells them to the highest bidder. I wouldn't exactly call him a good guy. And ArmaTech isn't the best place for a T-Rex to be walking around."

"Let's split up," Dynamo Joe says. "Madame Meteorite, you take Rolling Thunder and Robot X-treme to Mount Rushmore and knock those Pterodactyls out of the sky. Sunbolt and I will stop the Tyrannosaurus Rex."

"On it," Madam Meteorite says. "Take care, Eric."

[Farewell, Meta Zero unit,] Robot X-treme says.

"Be good," Rolling Thunder adds.

"You too," I say.

And then, they're gone.

"Here's the blindfold, Eric," Sunbolt says, wrapping it around my head. "Time to go."

She takes my hand and leads me back through a

door. I hear that wild disco music again as a series of latches close shut. Then, we're airborne.

"Are you sure you don't want me to drop you off somewhere?" she asks.

"No," I say. "Anywhere is fine."

A few minutes later, we touch down and she removes the blindfold. But as I open my eyes, I can't believe where we're standing.

"The police station?" I ask.

"We figured this was the safest place for you," Dynamo Joe says. "They're a great help for runaways."

"But I'm not a—."

"Good luck, Eric," Sunbolt says, shaking my hand. "But we've got to get to ArmaTech to stop a T-Rex."

"Take it easy, dude," Dynamo Joe says with a wink, "And don't lose that cool Halloween costume."

I was right! He was the guy from the store!

But before I can respond, Sunbolt takes off and Dynamo Joe follows with a tremendous jump.

They're gone.

I look back at the police station. Maybe I should go inside. After all, I am sort of a runaway. But I already know that no one inside that building can help me.

Nope. I need to help myself.

And I can start by finding the Time Trotter. Which means it's time for a second date with a T. Rex.

So, I tighten the straps on my Groovy Threads bag, stretch out my legs, and head for ArmaTech.

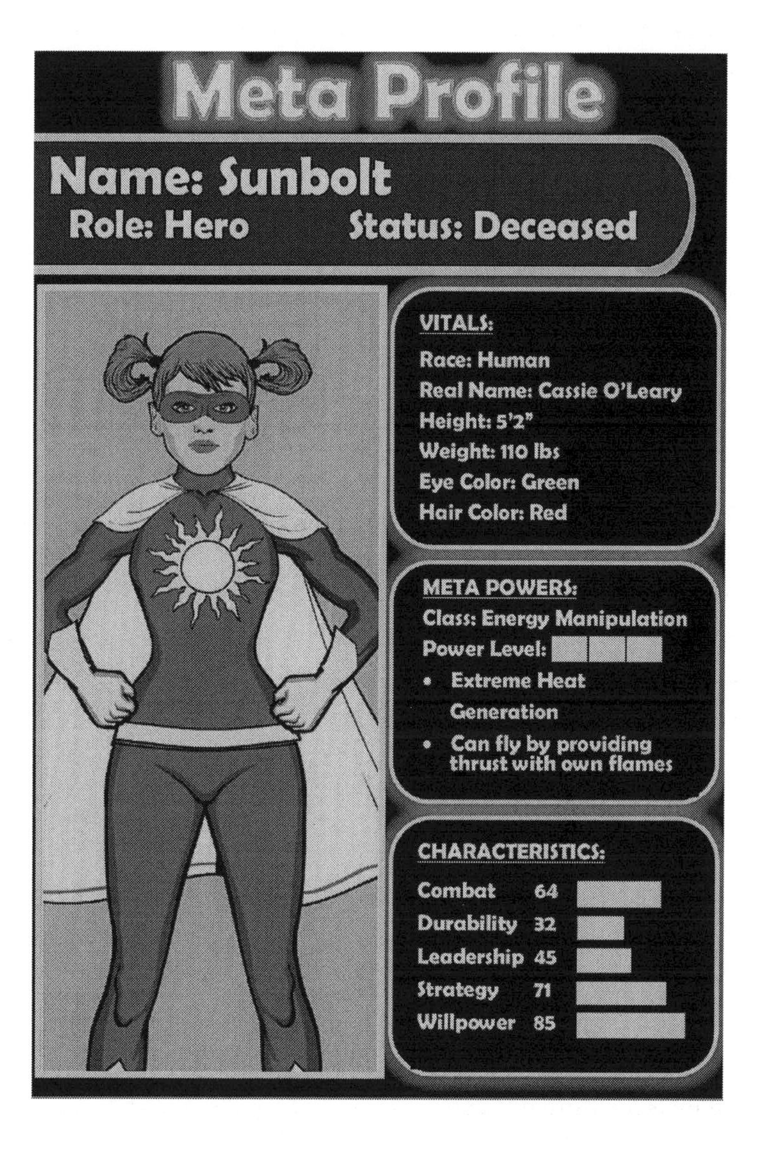
Meta Profile
Name: Sunbolt
Role: Hero
Status: Deceased
VITALS:
Race: Human
Real Name: Cassie O'Leary
Height: 5'2"
Weight: 110 lbs
Eye Color: Green
Hair Color: Red
META POWERS:
Class: Energy Manipulation
Power Level:
• Extreme Heat Generation
• Can fly by providing thrust with own flames
CHARACTERISTICS:
Combat 64
Durability 32
Leadership 45
Strategy 71
Willpower 85

SEVEN

I MAKE A STARTLING DISCOVERY

By the time I reach ArmaTech, I'm a sweaty mess.

Since I didn't have the luxury of travelling by Freedom Flyer, I literally had to cut through half the backyards in Keystone City to get here. But I'm lucky I made it all. I mean, who knew there were so many crazy dogs guarding their owner's property?

Note to self: never become a mailman.

The whole time I was kicking myself for not borrowing Sunbolt's flight power. But then again, she took off so fast I probably wouldn't have had time to do it anyway. Nevertheless, I'm here for my second run-in with a T-Rex.

And what sane person would want to miss that?

As I approach ArmaTech, I take cover in some nearby woods. The sky is pitch black and the only sounds I hear are crickets chirping and my feet crunching through the underbrush. So, in other words, it's pretty darn creepy out.

Awesome.

I look up at the ArmaTech building. It's a tall, windowless building sitting high atop a rocky cliff overlooking a lake. The only way in is a long, winding, single-lane road that leads right into a twenty-foot high chain-link fence covered in barbed wire. Next to the front gate is a guard station, but it looks empty.

In fact, the whole place seems empty.

But that's not all that's odd.

Why's it so darn quiet?

I mean, I was expecting to walk into a raging battle scene, but I don't see anyone.

Where's the T-Rex?

Or Sunbolt and Dynamo Joe?

Did they finish fighting already? I mean, I guess it's possible. It did take me a long time to get here. And if that's the case, I probably missed out on my one shot to nab the Time Trotter.

But something feels off.

I need to get closer, but there's a ton of open space between me and the chain-link fence. As soon as I step out of the woods, I'll be exposed for at least a hundred yards. So, I can either stay here safe and sound and wonder what happened, or I can go check it out for myself.

Whenever I'm faced with situations like this, I always ask myself: 'What would Shadow Hawk do?'

And then I usually wish I subbed in Dog-Gone.

Well, here goes nothing.

I take a deep breath, and then bolt as fast as I can up the winding road. I pray no one is watching from above because I figure I'm pretty hard to miss right now. It feels like forever, but when I finally reach the guard station I dive beneath the window.

I stay there for a few minutes and catch my breath. Since no one's attacked me yet, I figure I was right and the place is empty. But I need to be sure, so I pop up, peek inside the guard tower, and duck back down.

The coast is clear, and the side window is cracked open. If I'm going to get inside, I need to open the front gate. So, I open the window, hoist myself up, and roll inside, landing head first.

Well, that wasn't graceful.

I shake myself off and look at the control panel. There are two buttons, a green one and a red one. I don't think it's possible to overthink this, so I bash the green one. The front gate slides open with the loudest SCREECH I've ever heard in my life.

So much for the element of surprise.

Now I've got no choice but to go full throttle. I leap out of the guard station and run through the open gate when I realize something. There's no damage. I mean, normally you'd expect to see massive damage in a battle between Metas and a T-Rex. You know, things like crushed trucks, shattered windows, fallen lampposts.

But there's nothing.

It's like there was no fight at all.

I'm about to round the corner when I suddenly hear voices. I freeze.

"Did you find anything on your side of the building?" Dynamo Joe asks.

"Nope," Sunbolt says. "But the Nerve Center said a T-Rex was here. This is ArmaTech isn't it, Dad?"

"It sure is, dear," Dynamo Joe says.

Peering around the corner, I find Dynamo Joe and Sunbolt standing side by side. Dynamo Joe has his hands on his hips, while Sunbolt twirls a pigtail.

Well, I guess I'm not the only one confused around here. I mean, believe me, it's not like I want to see a T-Rex destroying things around here, but I was hoping to find the Time Trotter. He may be the only person who really knows what's going on.

So, now what?

I mean, I know I'm not supposed to interfere in events from the past, but now I've hit a total dead end. And the more I think about it, the more it seems like there's only one move left to make. I don't want to do it, but if I don't tell these heroes my real identity, I'm afraid I'll never figure out how to fix my problem.

I'm about to step out and reveal myself when—

"Dad!" Sunbolt says, pointing in the opposite direction. "I see something."

"Where?" Dynamo Joe says, moving next to her.

"Over there," she says. "In the bushes."

"Are you sure?" Dynamo Joe asks, racing towards the brush. "Because I don't see any—"

FZOOM!

Suddenly, there's a massive burst of light.

I turn away, just as a heat wave blankets my skin.

What's going on? No T. Rex I know can breathe fire.

But when I look back, I can't believe it.

Dynamo Joe is lying face down on the ground, and flames are dancing wildly around Sunbolt's fingers.

"Sorry, Dad," she says.

Wait, what?

I-I'm in shock.

Did she just take out her own father?

But… why?

And then it hits me.

The Trickster.

Sunbolt is the Trickster?

But it makes no sense. I mean, she just saved my life.

Why would she do this?

Then, Sunbolt looks my way and I pull back just in time. I can't let her see me. But when I peek around the corner I'm in for another shock, because Sunbolt scoops up Dynamo Joe and throws him over her shoulder like he weighs nothing!

How'd she do that? I don't remember reading anything about her having Super Strength?

But the surprises don't end there, because instead of flying away, Sunbolt carries Dynamo Joe towards the ArmaTech building. Suddenly, there's a loud CLICK, and a garage door slides open right in the side of the building, bathing them in light! Then, she walks inside, taking Dynamo Joe with her!

Huh?

Why is Sunbolt going inside ArmaTech? But before I can puzzle that one out, I hear another CLICK, and the door starts closing!

This time, I know exactly what Shadow Hawk would do. I sprint for the door and slide headfirst. My body hits the pavement hard, my momentum carrying me just beneath the door before it slams shut. I made it! But there's no time to pat myself on the back. I scramble to my feet and duck behind a large piece of equipment, hoping beyond hope she didn't see me.

I stay silent as I listen to Sunbolt's footsteps fading in the distance. My heart is beating a mile a minute, but I don't dare to move a muscle. I wait until I'm sure she's gone, and then I wait a few minutes more.

This was a huge risk. But I can't just let her take Dynamo Joe. Who knows what she'll do to him. Or what she's done to all the others.

Finally, I stand up and take a look around. To my surprise, it looks like I'm standing in a factory. The space is large and sterile-looking, with stark-white walls and white concrete floors. In the center of the room are several large vats with thick pipes running into the walls. Each vat is labeled with strange ingredients like: Nitric Acid, Chemical X, and Gamma Rays.

Note to self: stay clear of those.

I only see one way out, a corridor on the other side of the room. Clearly, that's where Sunbolt went. For a second, I consider turning back. I mean, who knows what I'll find in there? But I can't just leave Dynamo Joe.

So, I take a deep breath and cautiously enter the corridor. The white motif continues inside. I guess ArmaTech got a great deal on white paint. The corridor goes on for a while, and then I hit a fork in the road.

One passageway turns right and the other left. They both seem to go on for a while with no end in sight. I've got no clue which way to go, so I play eeny meeny miny moe. Left wins and fifty yards later it dawns on me that eeny meeny miny moe is probably not how Shadow Hawk makes his decisions.

Suddenly, the space opens up, and I'm standing in a huge chamber without windows or doors, except for the one I came in through. At first, I think I'm alone. But then, I realize I'm not.

Not by a longshot.

That's because the room is filled with animals—caged animals! There are dogs, cats, guinea pigs, and all sorts of other creatures. The weird thing is that none of them react to my presence. I look more closely into a dog cage and notice the animal is wearing a white tag around its neck.

But instead of a name, it says: #1974X.

Another dog has: #3721X.

That's strange.

What are those for?

I walk past a cage filled with mice. Actually, these guys look pretty big, so they're probably rats.

Then, I notice metal tables clustered in the center and rolling carts filled with surgical equipment. My first thought is that this must be a veterinary hospital.

But then I remember I'm inside ArmaTech.

So, this isn't a hospital.

It's… a lab!

My stomach turns.

They're experimenting on these animals!

My instincts tell me to throw open the cages and free them all, but I can't. I mean, who knows why they're here? Maybe they hold the secret to curing some future disease. I desperately want to believe it, but deep inside I know it's not true. These animals aren't here to help humanity. They're here for weapons testing.

I walk past another cart holding an array of vials. I read the labels: *Muscular Cell Decomposer. Molecule Reverser. Brain Growth Serum.*

I feel sick to my stomach.

As I continue on, I look at the animals more closely.

Cats are missing tufts of fur, and the dogs are so lethargic they don't even look my way.

I'm heartbroken.

There's nothing I can do, and I still have to find Sunbolt and Dynamo Joe. I need to get back on track. I wipe my eyes and get ready to split, when I hear—

"H-Help… m-me…"

I jump out of my skin. What's that?

As I spin around, I see a three-fingered hand wrapped around the cell bar of a prison door.

O.M.G!

There's a… a small person on his knees, staring at me with a pair of big, blue eyes.

"Help… me," he pleads.

And then I realize he's not a person at all.

He's an alien!

Meta Profile

Name: Dynamo Joe

Role: Hero **Status: Deceased**

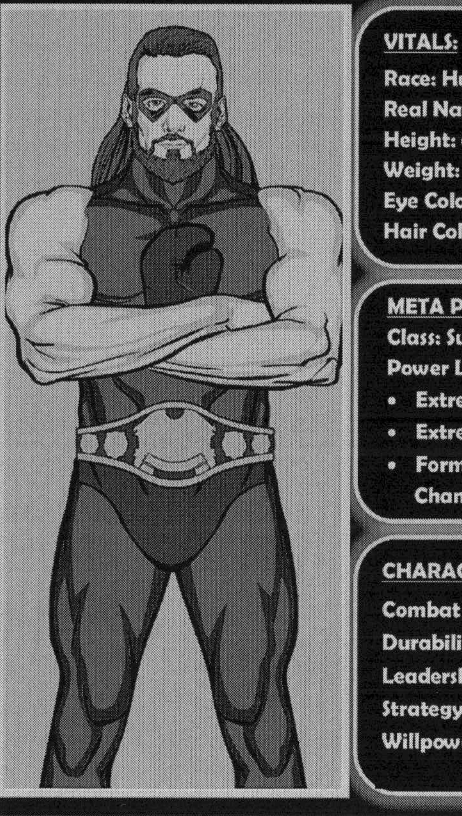

VITALS:

Race: Human
Real Name: Joseph O'Leary
Height: 6'2"
Weight: 270 lbs
Eye Color: Green
Hair Color: Brown

META POWERS:

Class: Super Strength
Power Level:

- Extreme Strength
- Extreme Agility
- Former Boxing Champion

CHARACTERISTICS:

Combat	95
Durability	90
Leadership	96
Strategy	85
Willpower	92

EIGHT

I GET SOME KEY INFORMATION

"Help… me."

I'm stunned.

There's an alien in a cell who's talking to me, but I'm so shocked I can't register a word he's saying. I mean, a minute ago I was looking for a T-Rex. Then, I discovered Sunbolt was the Trickster and followed her inside of ArmaTech where I stumbled upon an animal laboratory. The next thing I know, I'm face to face with an alien!

An alien, right here on Earth!

An alien from the past!

And that's probably not a good thing.

The poor guy is bent over, his pink, three-fingered hand wrapped around the cell bars. He's looking up at me with big, blue eyes, struggling to breathe. He's small, smaller than me, and dressed in a tattered blue uniform with yellow stripes on his shoulders. His outfit sort of reminds me of the army, where the number of stripes on a uniform signifies rank.

"P-Please…," he pleads. "F-Free me."

"Free you?" I say, finally managing to find my voice. "I don't even know you." He doesn't look like any alien I've seen before. And trust me, I've seen lots of aliens. But before I'd even consider helping him, there's one thing I need to know—is he a good guy or a bad guy?

"I-I am from far away," he says, peering up at the ceiling. "I must get back… get help." Just then, his hand slips and he tumbles to the ground.

He lands hard, coughing like a maniac. That's when I spot red slashes on his ribs, like he was scratched by a tiger, and a horrible thought crosses my mind.

"Are they experimenting on you?" I ask.

"They can do as they wish," he spits. "But they will learn the will of an Intergalactic Paladin is unbreakable."

"An Intergalactic what?" I ask.

"Not 'what,'" he wheezes, struggling to sit up. "But 'who.' The Intergalactic Paladins are…," then he bends over and hacks again.

Man, he doesn't look so good.

"Pardon me," he says, wiping some gunk from his chin. "The Intergalactic Paladins are the protectors of the cosmos. We patrol the farthest regions of space, defending the innocent from the direst of threats."

"Really?" I say, scratching my head. I've never heard of the Intergalactic Paladins before, but they certainly sound like good guys.

"My name is, um, Eric," I say. "What's yours?"

"I am called Proog," he says.

"Nice to meet you, Proog," I say. "But, if you don't mind me asking, how did you end up in here? I mean, what were you protecting Earth from?"

"I was not just protecting Earth, young one," Proog says, looking me dead on. "But saving the universe."

"The universe?" I say. "Wow, that's a pretty tall order. And what exactly were you saving it from?"

But instead of answering, he looks me up and down with his bug-like eyes, and suddenly I feel uncomfortable. It's like he's reading my soul, determining if I'm worthy of being told or not.

Finally, he leans forward and says, "from Krule."

"Krule?" I repeat. "Who's Krule?"

"He is known by many names," Proog says. "Krule the Tyrant, Krule the Wretched, but most notably, Krule the Conqueror."

"Well, he sure sounds like a man with many talents," I say. "Please, send him my congrats on that, but let him know there's no need to thank me in person. Like, ever."

"Hopefully, you will never meet him in person," Proog says. "Because before I was ambushed and trapped in this filthy prison, I ensured his fate by hiding the key to his freedom."

I clean out my ears.

"Um, sorry," I say, "But I couldn't help but notice you said the word 'key.' Do you mean, like, a Cosmic Key kind of a key?"

"Yes!" Proog says, his eyes bulging out of his skull. "How do you know of the Cosmic Key?"

"Well, it's kind of a long story," I say. "But to cut to the chase, I saw an image of a man with three-eyes and red skin. He said he wanted the Cosmic Key."

"But that's not possible," Proog says, clearly alarmed.

"Okay," I say. "But I'm positive I saw what I saw."

"Then the person you describe was no ordinary man," Proog says. "It was Krule the Conqueror himself. But how did he know the key was here?"

"Beats me," I ask. "But if that was Krule, why's he after the Cosmic Key anyway?"

"Because he is also a prisoner," he says. "Trapped with his army of ingrates in the 13th Dimension. And only the Cosmic Key can let him out."

Then it hits me.

The Cosmic Key!

Everything that's happened to me revolves around this Cosmic Key!

I mean, that's what Krule was using the Time Trotter to find. That's the reason my timestream is all screwed up! That's the reason I'm stuck here in the past!

But I feel like I've been in this movie before. I know there's got to be more to the story.

"Can we rewind a second?" I ask. "What the heck is the 13th Dimension, and how come the Cosmic Key is the only thing that can let him out?"

"The 13th Dimension is a special pocket in space," Proog says, "existing outside the space-time continuum. It was discovered centuries ago by my forefathers, and we have used it ever since to humanely contain the most dangerous criminals in the universe. You see, the Intergalactic Paladins are sworn to protect, not to destroy. Using the 13th Dimension as our prison allows us to remove criminal threats without ever breaking our vows. Once inside, the powers of the prisoners are neutralized."

Wow, that's pretty wild.

"The Cosmic Key is the only object that can unlock the door to the 13th Dimension," he continues. "But using the 13th Dimension is also a double-edged sword. It will trap criminals forever, but once inside, they will never grow old."

"Whoa!" I say, my mind blown. "So, you're saying all of the criminals in there will live forever? Like, they'll never die?"

"Precisely," he says.

Well, scratch that family vacation to the 13th Dimension! Then, I remember Krule saying he knows the Cosmic Key was once here on Earth. In fact, he said he could feel its energy. So, he was right!

Suddenly, an image of the Orb of Oblivion flashes in my mind and I shudder. I've had enough run-ins with crazy extraterrestrial objects to know that this Cosmic Key is probably more than it seems.

"So, let me get this straight," I say. "Krule, one of the most heinous dudes in the galaxy, is trapped in the 13th Dimension looking for the Cosmic Key. And, for some reason, you decided to hide this puppy right here on Earth? Why us? Aren't there, like, millions of other planets you could have stuck it on?"

"Yes, but very few have the Meta energy of Earth," Proog says. "You see, the Cosmic Key has a conscience of its own."

Of course it does.

"You see, the Cosmic Key cannot be contained," Proog continues. "It is attracted to Meta energy, and your planet emits one of the highest concentrations of Meta energy in the galaxy. We believed that if we buried it here it would stay here, instead of wandering through space in search of Meta energy where it could fall into the wrong hands. Fortunately, I succeeded in the first part of my mission, but I could not escape before being ambushed and losing my Infinity Wand."

Infinity Wand? What's that?

But before I can ask, I hear voices!

It's Sunbolt! And a man!

"Run," Proog whispers.

I can't just leave him here. I look around for something to unlock the cell door, but I don't see anything. The voices are getting closer! I'm too late!

"I've got to hide," I whisper. "Don't give me away."

As I look around for somewhere to hide, I hear—

"You collect more heroes," the man says. "I'll see what I can learn from our special guest."

Uh oh! He's coming in here! I'm trapped!

I duck behind the dog cages. This is not good. I mean, how am I going to get out of here?

"Don't worry, Fairchild," Sunbolt says. "I've got three more in mind."

Fairchild? Isn't that the owner of ArmaTech? And did she just say three more?

O.M.G!

She's going for Rolling Thunder, Madame Meteorite, and Robot X-Treme! I've got to warn them!

Suddenly, I hear footsteps running the opposite way. That's got to be Sunbolt! I have to stop her!

But before I can move, Fairchild enters the lab!

I hold my breath.

Suddenly, I hear CLANKING. Peering over the cage, I see Fairchild. He has his back to me, but I can make out some of his features. He's tall, with dark hair and broad shoulders. It looks like he's assembling some kind of a pole with a sharp tip on it, like a spear.

"Good afternoon," Fairchild says. "Shall we continue our interview?"

He must be talking to Proog!

I'm not sure what to do. I could help Proog, but I'll lose time warning the others about Sunbolt.

But I can't just let Fairchild hurt Proog.

Decision made!

But as soon as I stand up, Proog meets my eyes and shakes his head from side to side. What? Is he saying he doesn't want my help? But I can't just leave him here. And even if I wanted to go, there's no way to sneak out without being seen.

Then, I feel something tugging my leg!

I look down to see a gray-and-black German Shepherd appear out of thin air!

It's that invisible dog!

And he's pulling my bell bottom pants!

What's he doing here?

The dog looks at me, and I mouth: '*What?*'

"Now," Fairchild says, approaching Proog with his spear. "Let's pick up where we left off. Tell me where you hid the Cosmic Key?"

I want to help Proog, but the dog is pulling me across the room! Then, the mutt releases me and runs to the back wall. And that's when I notice the hole behind a loose panel.

It's an escape route!

So, that's how he got inside.

The dog nods his head, and then squeezes through, disappearing from sight.

I hear a SCREECH.

Fairchild opened Proog's cell!

If I'm going to help Proog, it's now or never.

"Go!" Proog commands.

I freeze. Wait, is he yelling at me, or Fairchild?

"So, he speaks," Fairchild says. "This is a much better start than our last session."

"Go!" Proog yells again.

This time, there's no mistaking it. He's yelling at me!

I want to help, but he's clearly telling me not to.

I'm paralyzed. I don't know what to do.

"Now!" Proog orders.

Why doesn't he want my help?

I feel crummy, but I drop to my hands and knees, crawl through the hole, and I'm gone.

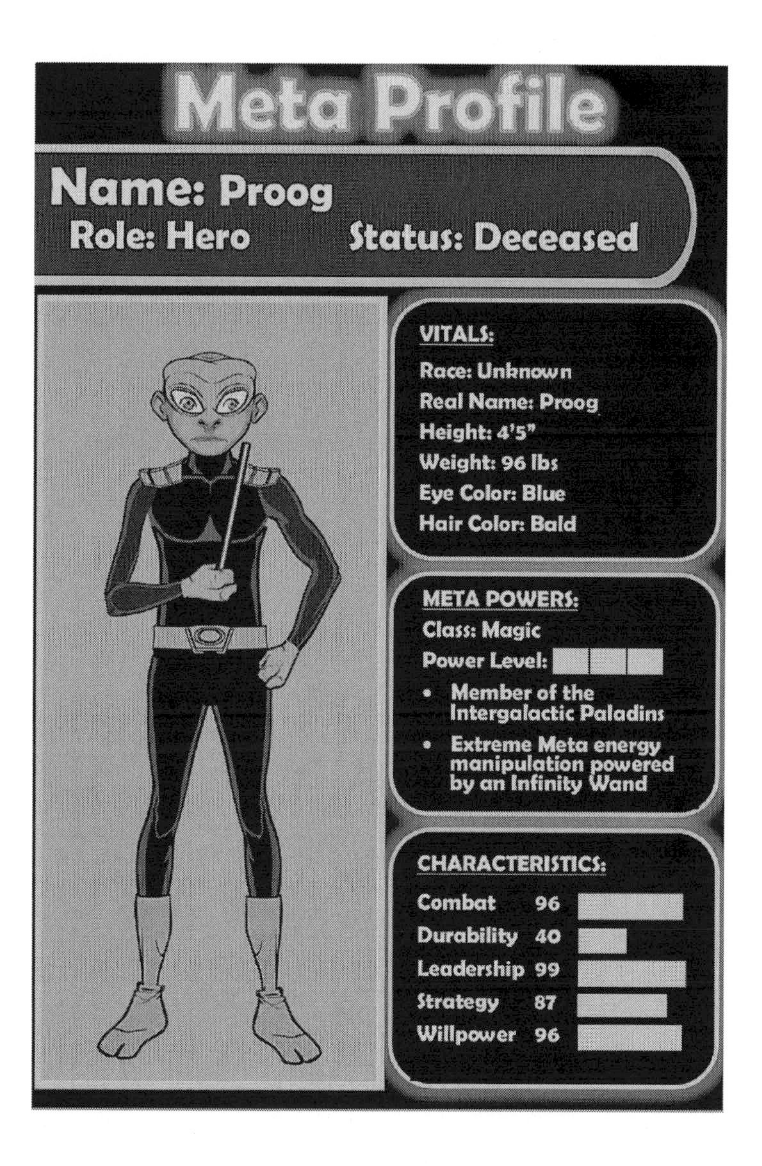
Meta Profile
Name: Proog
Role: Hero
Status: Deceased
VITALS:
Race: Unknown
Real Name: Proog
Height: 4'5"
Weight: 96 lbs
Eye Color: Blue
Hair Color: Bald
META POWERS:
Class: Magic
Power Level:
• Member of the Intergalactic Paladins
• Extreme Meta energy manipulation powered by an Infinity Wand
CHARACTERISTICS:
Combat 96
Durability 40
Leadership 99
Strategy 87
Willpower 96

NINE

I MAKE A QUICK CHANGE

By the time I reach the woods, I'm a total basket case.

My furry companion is waiting for me by a tree, but as soon as I catch up, I collapse onto the grass. I can barely catch my breath, but that's not why I'm so upset.

I mean, what kind of a hero am I? I basically just left Proog behind to get tortured. I feel lower than low. But what choice did I have? Proog basically ordered me to leave. And there's nothing I can do about it now.

But I can't just leave him there. I swear I'll be back to help him if it's the last thing I do. But first I need to take care of some other business—like stopping Sunbolt.

I still can't believe she's the Trickster. It just doesn't make sense. I mean, she saved my life, so why is she doing this?

But I can't figure that out now. I need to warn the other heroes before it's too late. After all, if she took down her own father, there's no telling what she'll do to them. Then, I hear scratching by the tree.

I'm such a heel. I forgot to thank my rescuer.

"Hey, thanks," I say, looking over at my new dog buddy. "I appreciate you—"

Then, I realize something.

My furry companion isn't a 'he.' She's a 'she!'

Well, that's awkward.

But she doesn't seem to mind because she lowers her head and nuzzles my arm. She's a little shorter than Dog-Gone, but with gray and black fur. I look at the tag on her collar. It reads: *GG.*

GG?

Her tag is black, which is different than the white tags the other animals had in the lab.

"You're not from the lab, are you?" I ask.

She shakes her head from side to side which I'm taking as a firm 'no.'

"So, what were you doing in there?"

She bares her teeth and growls.

"Whoa, it's okay," I say, trying to calm her down. "There's nothing dangerous here. It's cool."

She stops growling, lowers her head, and whimpers.

Clearly something at ArmaTech agitated her. I wonder what it could be?

"Do you need a hug?"

She comes close and I wrap my arms around her. It's nice to feel the warmth of a furry friend again, even if it's not my own.

"I guess I should call you something. Your tag says GG. Hey, how about Gigi?"

She licks my chin, making me laugh.

Okay, that's settled. But then I realize something.

Invisible dogs aren't a dime a dozen.

This pooch must be one of Dog-Gone's ancestors!

I'm too far back in history for her to be his mom, but maybe she's his grandma, or his great grandma. I'd love nothing more than to tell her all about her descendent, but I know I can't do that either. After all, I'd hate for something to happen to my future furball.

"So, I'm guessing you made that hole we escaped from, didn't you? You sure are a brave one. Clearly, your gene pool got diluted as it went down the line."

She licks my nose.

As nice as it is to just hang out and take a breather, I know we can't stay here. I've got to find the other heroes before Sunbolt does. The problem is that Sunbolt blindfolded me when she took me to their secret headquarters. So, I've got no clue where to go. But maybe my companion knows!

"Gigi, do you know where to find Rolling Thunder, Madame Meteorite, or Robot X-treme?" I ask.

But she just looks at me and scratches behind her ear. Okay, that's a negative.

Time to think. Even though I was blindfolded, were there any clues that could help me pinpoint the location of the Nerve Center? Well, I remember Sunbolt unlatching a bunch of locks to the outside door. But there must be millions of doors with locks in Keystone City.

I try to remember any other clues, but I come up empty. It's time to face the music, I've got no idea where—

Wait a minute!

Music.

Music!

There was music playing when we entered and left the Nerve Center! Disco music!

Then, I realize something.

Disco music was also playing when I entered Groovy Threads. And Dynamo Joe was the shopkeeper at Groovy Threads.

Coincidence?

Maybe. But maybe not.

"Follow me, Gigi," I say, scrambling to my feet. "It's time to boogie!"

***

It's morning by the time we reach Main Street.

The air is chilly and the sun is rising slowly, like it's deciding if it wants to wake up or hit the snooze button. The street is empty, except for a few shopkeepers busy opening their stores. In other words, the conditions are perfect for breaking into a fine clothing establishment.

Gigi and I stay out of sight as we make our way to Groovy Threads. I've had plenty of time to map out our strategy, and I'm pretty sure the secret entrance to the Nerve Center won't be through the front door. So, if I were a gambling man, I'd say our best bet is around back.

We sneak down the alleyway to the rear of the store when I find something I'm not expecting.

The back door is wide open.

In fact, it's blown completely off its hinges!

Looking down, I see broken latches scattered at my feet. I bend over for a closer look and realize the latches aren't just broken, they're gnarled and twisted, like they've been melted. Well, I don't need to be a detective to figure this one out.

Sunbolt was here!

"Hey, girl," I whisper to Gigi. "I'll understand if you don't want to stick around."

But, to my surprise, Gigi let's out a low growl, steps inside the building, and turns invisible. How Dog-Gone is related to her is beyond me.

I follow her inside and hear the faint sound of music—disco music! Yep, we've come to the right place.

We're standing in a small hallway facing two closed doors. The door to our left reads: *Groovy Threads Storage Room.* The door to our right reads: *Electric Room. Danger: No Entry.*

Bingo. Right it is.

I turn the knob and the door swings open with ease.

But when I look inside, my eyes pop out of their sockets, because I can't believe what I'm seeing.

The Nerve Center looks like a war zone!

Monitors are shattered, consoles are crushed, and the giant conference table is split in two. There's debris as far as the eye can see, from computer parts to coffee mugs. But Sunbolt and the heroes are nowhere to be found.

Gigi runs over to a pile of rubble and barks. We dig through it, until we uncover something long and metallic. At first, I don't know what it is.

Then, it hits me.

It's Robot X-treme's arm!

I plop down on the ground with my head in my hands. I'm too late! Sunbolt got them!

I feel terrible for Rolling Thunder, Madame Meteorite, and Robot X-treme. They probably had no clue Sunbolt was the Trickster. I remember Dynamo Joe saying: *all of the people we trust are right here in this room.*

So much for trust.

Now they're all captured.

I feel totally deflated. Like I let them all down.

Sunbolt has probably taken them back to ArmaTech by now. But why? What is Fairchild doing with them?

And what am I supposed to do now?

I wish my family was here.

Wait.

My family!

If I can find Mom and Dad, they can help me break into ArmaTech and figure out what's going on. But how am I going to do that? Then, my eyes land on a squat computer that somehow managed to survive the carnage.

It's their Meta Monitor!

I hop over the shattered conference table and check it out. The screen is cracked, but it still looks operational! I type into the keyboard: *Display Meta Signatures.*

The console spits back: *Error.*

Error! Okay, don't panic. I've got to remember this isn't the sophisticated system I'm used to. Let's try something simpler. I type: *Meta Powers.*

Error.

Okay, now I'm getting annoyed. How am I supposed to find Mom or Dad if I can't track their power signatures? This computer may be advanced for this timestream, but it's nothing like TechnocRat built.

Then, I remember something.

This system wasn't built by TechnocRat.

It was built by Robot X-treme.

I type in: *Find Meta 3 Units.*

Suddenly, the screen comes alive with blips.

Yes!

Except there are hundreds of them, scattered all over the globe. Since every blip represents a Meta 3, I need to narrow the scope. So, I move the cursor over the United

States, find Keystone City, and click. The monitor zooms in again, pulling up an overhead of the city.

This time there are way fewer blips—five to be exact. I click on them one by one. With every click, I get a brief description of the power signature identified.

Meta 3 Unit: Super-speed. Nope.

Meta 3 Unit: Meta-morph. Nope again.

Meta 3 Unit: Psychic.

Psychic!

I home in on the signature. It's coming from the Keystone City Library. That's right! Mom told me she used to work at the library before becoming a full-time Meta hero. That's across from the police station.

Okay, let's check out those other two blips.

Meta 3 Unit: Super-Intelligence. Clearly not Dad.

Meta 3 Unit: Super-Strength.

Winner, winner, chicken dinner!

The signal is coming from the Keystone City Police Station. Well, Dad was on the police force before becoming the Warden of Lockdown.

"Come on, Gigi!"

We dash out of the Nerve Center and back into the hallway. But before we step out, I stop myself. I can't go rushing over to my parents like this. I was lucky my folks didn't study my face the first time, but this time there's no way to avoid it—and that could destroy the future!

Then, my eyes fall on the door across the hall: *Groovy Threads Storage Room.* Hmmm. Maybe there's something in there I can use to cover my face. Like a hat.

The door opens into a dark room. I fumble along the wall until I find the light switch and flick it on, revealing racks of clothing. Yes, I was right!

But as I step inside, I do a double take, because they aren't regular clothes at all. They're Meta costumes!

I move down the line, running my hand through dozens of backup uniforms for Dynamo Joe, Rolling Thunder, and Madame Meteorite. At the end of the rack are a bunch of smaller costumes in different colors—blue and red, black and gray, red and white. There's a paper pinned to one of the costumes that reads: *New Sunbolt Designs—Must be Tailored.*

Then, I get an idea.

I put down my Groovy Threads bag and look through the selection. If I can fit into one of these costumes, then I can hide my real identity from my parents! The black and gray one looks the largest, so I pull it off its hangar. I'm about to try it on when I find a pair of eyes staring at me.

"Um, do you mind, Gigi?"

Gigi rolls her eyes and spins around.

I take off my clothes and step into the costume. It's a little tighter than I'm used to, but it fits. I jump up and down a few times, trying to stretch it out.

Now I just need shoes and a mask.

I spot some cardboard boxes across the room. I open the first one which is filled with boots. I sift through, looking for my size, but the only ones that look close are neon green. I try them on and they fit perfectly.

Well, I won't be winning any Meta fashion awards.

I open another box filled with gloves, and another stuffed with belts. Still no masks. One box left.

I say a prayer and pop it open.

It's filled with helmets. Loads of freaking helmets.

My heart sinks. This isn't what I wanted at all. I pull a few out. There's one shaped like an army helmet, and another like a construction helmet.

I'm about to close the box when I spot something interesting. One of the helmets looks like it's from the medieval ages. I always loved knights, but as I pull it out, the visor slams down on my fingers. Ouch!

I'm about to toss it when I realize something. The visor could cover my face. If my noggin fits into this thing, my parents won't see my features at all!

I put the helmet over my head and push it down, lowering the visor. Wow, it's snug. But it's also really hard to see out the sides. I don't know how knights fought in these things. It's not ideal, but it's my only option.

"Let's go, Gigi," I say. "We've got heroes to save!"

But as we run out, I smash headfirst into the wall.

Freaking visor!

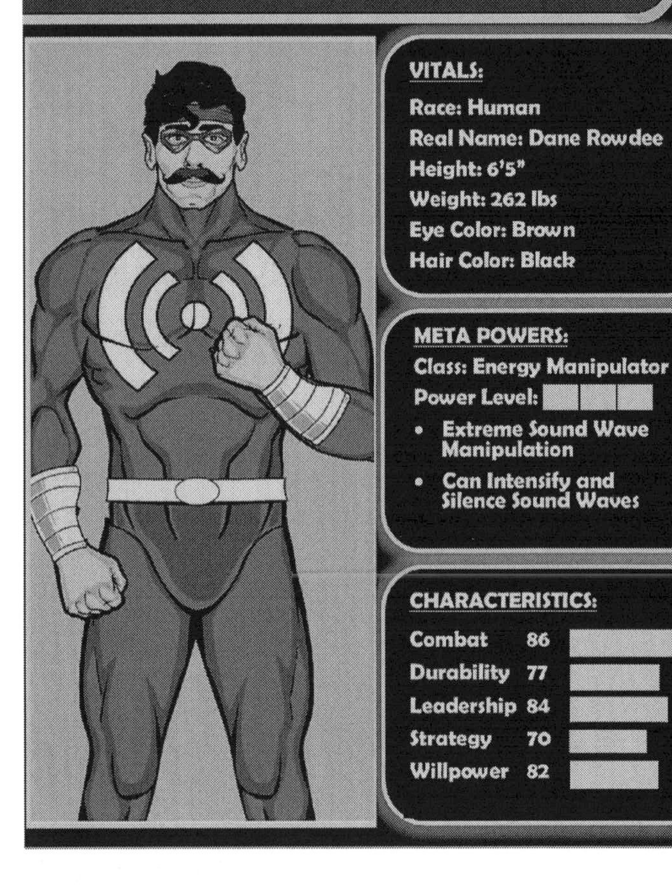
Meta Profile
Name: Rolling Thunder
Role: Hero
Status: Deceased
VITALS:
Race: Human
Real Name: Dane Rowdee
Height: 6'5"
Weight: 262 lbs
Eye Color: Brown
Hair Color: Black
META POWERS:
Class: Energy Manipulator
Power Level:
Extreme Sound Wave Manipulation
Can Intensify and Silence Sound Waves
CHARACTERISTICS:
Combat 86
Durability 77
Leadership 84
Strategy 70
Willpower 82

TEN

I AMBUSH MY PARENTS

Guess who's back at the police station.

I don't know why I keep ending up here, but maybe somebody's trying to tell me something—like I'd be better off behind bars. I have to admit, right now it sounds appealing. You know, like playing Monopoly where you can just chill out in jail until you roll doubles.

Unfortunately, I don't have time to relax. If I'm going to save Proog and the other heroes, I need to get moving. So, this trip to the police station isn't exactly a social visit. I'm here for serious business.

I'm here to recruit Dad.

The good news is that I'm well-disguised, especially wearing my helmet. I've also rehearsed what I'm going to say about a million times. So, I'm as prepared as I'm going to get. Now it's time to execute the plan. Gigi and I just need to walk in, grab him, and go.

This should be a piece of cake.

But as we push open the double doors, I realize finding Dad might be a lot harder than I thought. That's because the inside of the police station is a zoo. Every inch of the ginormous space seems to be occupied by someone—from cops booking criminals to a grandma filing a missing cat report. The noise level is deafening, like a loud buzz, but you can't really make out a single conversation. The whole scene is pure sensory overload.

And to top it off, I don't see Dad anywhere.

As we approach the front desk, an officer with glasses looks up from his paper and says, "The Wizard of Oz is playing up the street, kid. This is the police station."

"Yes, we know it's the police station," I say. "We're looking for Officer Harkness."

"Officer who?" he says.

"Officer Harkness," I repeat. "Officer Tom Harkness."

"Tom Harkness?" he says, confused. Then, the lightbulb goes off. "Oh, you mean, Tommy Harkness?"

"Yes," I say. "Is he here?"

The cop chuckles and calls over his shoulder, "Hey, Sal! Get this. This kid wants to see 'Officer' Tommy Harkness! Isn't that a riot?"

"What's so funny?" I ask.

"Nothing," the cop says, wiping tears from his eyes.

"Go ahead. You'll find him in the back. He's on official mop-up duty."

But as we pass by, he's still laughing to himself.

"Official mop-up duty," he says. "I kill myself."

What's his problem?

Gigi and I weave through the crowd. I don't remember the police station being this crowded before. It's like all the whackos came out at once.

Suddenly, there's RAPPING on my helmet.

I spin around to find a skinny man with a thin moustache sitting in a chair. He's wearing a green suit and his left arm is handcuffed to a desk.

Gigi bares her teeth and growls.

"Easy, girl," I say, putting my hand on her neck.

"Riddle me this," the man says, "Why were the Middle Ages called the Dark Ages?"

"Um, I don't know," I say.

"Because there were too many knights!" he finishes, and then bursts out in maniacal laughter.

"Good one," I say. "You have a great day."

"You too," he says.

Note to self: stay out of prison.

Finally, we reach the back of the station, but I don't see Dad anywhere. In fact, there's nobody here but us and a blond-haired janitor who's… mopping up the floor.

No. Way.

"Um, excuse me," I say. "Are you Tom Harkness?"

The janitor lifts his head and I'm staring into a pair

of familiar blue eyes. It's Dad!

"Yeah," Dad says. "Who are you? And why are you dressed like that?"

Great questions, but ones that I'm ready for. All I need to do now is unleash my brilliant speech and Dad will be on our side.

"I'm a superhero," I say confidently. "And here's the deal. I know who the Trickster is, and I know where she's holding the missing heroes. But it's a dangerous mission and I can't rescue them alone. You're one of the greatest Meta's alive and I'll need your help."

Dad stops mopping and looks me up and down.

"Get lost, kid," he says. "I don't know what you're talking about."

Well, I wasn't expecting that.

Clearly, speechwriting isn't in my future.

I've got one shot to lay it all out there.

"Look," I say, "I know you're really Liberty Lad, a Meta 3 Super-strongman who's nearly invulnerable. I also know you're a champion of justice and a major germaphobe."

Dad looks down at his mop and then back at me. Then, he says, "How do you know all that stuff about me? Are you a psychic, because I hate psychics?"

"Um, no," I say. "Let's just say I have my methods. And I thought you were a police officer?"

"I will be," he says. "I'm working to save up enough money to take the police academy exam."

"Ah," I say. "Right." Then, I look at his young face again. I totally forgot he probably just graduated from high school! "Well, I'm pretty sure you'll be a great cop when you get there. So, what do you say? Will you help me? Pretty please with sprinkles on top?"

"Help you," he says. "I don't even know you. What's your name anyway?"

Great question. Hadn't thought of that one.

"I'm… the Nullifier," I say. "And this is… Fur-Begone."

"The Nullifier and Fur-Begone?" he says. "And you say you know who the Trickster is, huh? So, tell me, who is it? Maybe it's you?"

Here comes the moment of truth.

"No, it's not me," I say. "It's Sunbolt."

"Sunbolt?" he says, skeptically. "Really?"

"Really," I say. "And she's captured Dynamo Joe, Rolling Thunder, Madam Meteorite, and Robot X-treme."

"Hang on," he says. "Blue Bolt told me she was meeting up with Sunbolt and Master Mime."

"Aren't they missing also?" I ask.

"Yeah," he says. "They are. Okay, kid. Meet me out back in two minutes. I've got to put away some cleaning supplies." Then, he shoots us a determined look and heads off.

As Gigi and I exit through the rear door, I'm feeling pretty good about myself. It actually looks like part one of my plan might be a success. But I'm not so sure about part two.

Dad said he hates psychics, so if I tell him we still need to recruit Mom, he might bail on me. After all, they weren't exactly BFF's when those thugs held me hostage. I'll need to handle this very, very carefully. But I don't have much time either.

Speaking of time, where's Dad? We've been standing out here for more than a few minutes, and by the way Gigi is tapping her tail, she's clearly losing her patience.

Suddenly, a figure leaps out of the bushes, scaring us silly. It's Dad, in full superhero costume.

"What took you so long?" I ask.

"Sorry," he says. "Changing in the car is harder than I thought. Where are we going anyway?"

"To ArmaTech," I say.

"ArmaTech?" he says. "Don't they produce military weapons? If our friends are trapped there, it could be bad news?"

"Yeah," I say. "So, we've got to be ready for anything. Which is why we need to stop by the library."

"The library?" he says. "Don't you think now isn't the best time to check out a book?"

"Oh, no, we're not checking out a book," I say. "We're borrowing a superhero."

***

I spot Mom in the stacks, unloading a cart of books onto the shelves. It's weird seeing her so young. I mean, she's my Mom, but I'd recognize those eyes anywhere. She clearly doesn't see me, because as soon as some kids go by, she furrows her brow and the books fly into place all on their own.

I feel like I made the right decision coming here alone. Based on how she and Dad bickered the last time they were together, bringing him along would be risky. So, since dogs aren't allowed in the library, I asked him to keep an eye on Gigi for me. I can't say Gigi was thrilled about it, but I'll deal with that later.

I take a deep breath. I have the feeling recruiting Mom is going to be a lot harder than recruiting Dad. Plus, she's a psychic which means she could potentially read my mind at any time.

Fortunately, I've got powers of my own.

I concentrate hard and project an aura of negation around me. That should block her from penetrating my mind. I just need to stay on my toes because if my concentration slips for a second, she could find out I'm her kid from the future, blowing the whole thing.

I hide behind a bookshelf until some students leave the area. Then, I lower my visor and make my move.

"Excuse me, Kate." I say.

"It's Katie," she says absently. "How can I help—," but when she looks my way, she does a double take. "Um, do I know you?"

"No," I say. "But I know you, and I need Brainstorm's help."

"Brainstorm?" she says, looking around nervously. "What are you talking about?"

"It's okay," I say. "I didn't mean to startle you, but there's no time for games. We need to act fast. Lives are in danger—including Blue Bolt and Master Mime."

"Really?" she says. Then, she grabs my shoulders and pulls me into the stacks. "Okay, pipsqueak," she commands, "spill it. Who are you and what do you know about Blue Bolt and Master Mime?"

Then, her eyebrows go up.

"Why can't I get a read on you?" she asks. "Are you a psychic?"

Whew! My powers are working.

"No, I'm the Nullifier," I say, mustering up more confidence this time. "Look, it doesn't matter how I know who you are. You don't have to worry. Your secret is safe with me."

"And why should I trust you?" she asks. "Blue Bolt and Master Mime trusted the Trickster and look where it got them. Maybe you're the Trickster?"

"No," I say. "I'm a hero, just like you. And you're just gonna have to trust me. Look, I know who the real Trickster is, and I'll tell you, but I need you to join me… and a few other heroes… to save our friends. Deal?"

"Okay, kid," she says, crossing her arms. "I'll do anything to save my friends. Now tell me, who's the

Trickster?"

***

Yes! After explaining everything to Mom, which took way longer than even I expected, she's on board! Now I've got both of my parents helping me. The only wrinkle is that each doesn't know about the other. So, this could either be great, or it could be a bigger disaster then when Dog-Gone got into our bubble gum supply.

Since Mom needed a minute to get into costume, I told her I'd meet her outside. That's where I find Dad and Gigi sitting on a bench. For some reason, he doesn't look happy.

"You know," he says, "you forgot to mention your dog can turn invisible."

"Well," I say, "she's not really my—"

"So, I turn around and she's gone," he says. "I didn't know if she ran away or what. So, I'm running around looking for her like a fool, and then poof, she magically appears on the bench. I'm pretty sure she was sitting here watching me the whole time."

"Oh, sorry," I say. "Bad girl, Fur-Begone."

Gigi yawns.

"Anyway," he says, "where's this big superhero you needed to get?"

"Okay, Nullifier," Mom says, running down the walkway. "I'm ready to—," then she stops and looks at

Dad.

"Seriously?" Dad says. "Her?"

"He's the 'other hero?'" Mom asks.

"Hang on," I interject. "We're all heroes here."

"I can't work with her," Dad says, standing up.

"I refuse to work with that ignoramus," Mom says.

"How dare you!" Dad says. "I'm no ignoramus!"

Then, he leans over and whispers, "What's an ignoramus?"

I have no clue, but this is getting out of hand.

"Guys, stop," I say. "Listen we need to work together."

"No dice," Dad says. "I'm out."

"Ditto," Mom says, turning away. "Later, pipsqueak."

"Wait!" I call out.

But they don't stop.

They just keep walking away.

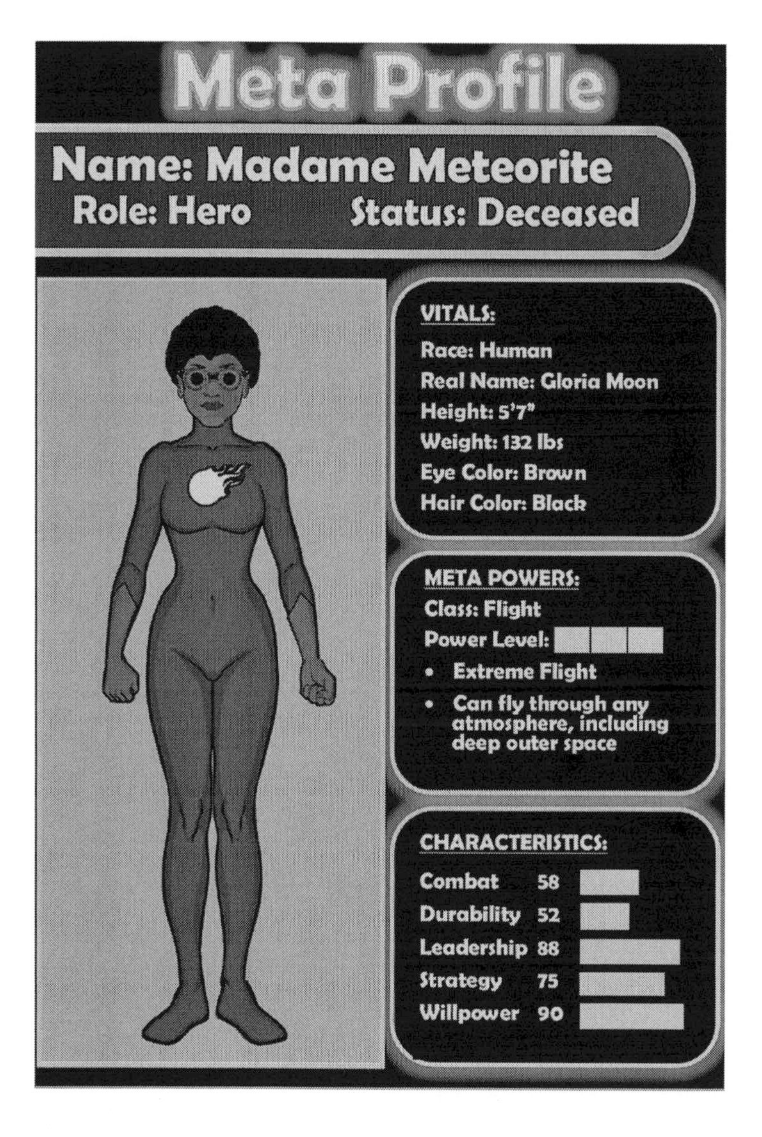
Meta Profile
Name: Madame Meteorite
Role: Hero
Status: Deceased
VITALS:
Race: Human
Real Name: Gloria Moon
Height: 5'7"
Weight: 132 lbs
Eye Color: Brown
Hair Color: Black
META POWERS:
Class: Flight
Power Level:
• Extreme Flight
• Can fly through any atmosphere, including deep outer space
CHARACTERISTICS:
Combat 58
Durability 52
Leadership 88
Strategy 75
Willpower 90

ELEVEN

I GET THE GANG BACK TOGETHER

This is getting ridiculous.

I mean, in my timestream my parents are happily married and spend loads of time together. But here, they hate each other so much they can't even share the same space. And now they're both walking away despite the monumental task before us.

Is this how they really treated each other in the past?

Or did Krule alter things so much there's no hope of bringing them back together?

And if that's the case, what happens to me?

In the future I won't even exist!

Okay, I know I'm not supposed to interfere, but now I've got no choice. I need to solve this once and for all.

"Stop!" I yell at the top of my lungs.

Surprisingly, they stop.

Dad looks over his shoulder, while Mom crosses her arms and taps her foot.

Wow. Okay, the floor is mine.

"Listen," I say. "I know you guys don't get along, but honestly, I don't know why. Liberty Lad, despite your unfortunate haircut, you're a good guy at heart who always fights for what's right. And Brainstorm, while you may have the worst superhero name of all time, you're a hero to the core with more willpower in your little pinkie than anyone I know. There's no reason you guys shouldn't get along. In fact, if you worked together, you'd be the best crime-fighting duo on the entire freaking planet."

Dad raises an eyebrow as Mom uncrosses her arms.

They're listening! I need to keep going.

"And let's not forget," I continue, "that Blue Bolt and Master Mime, your mutual friends, need your help. Not to mention all of the other heroes being held captive. I'm telling you, something dark is going on at ArmaTech. And if Sunbolt and Fairchild took out all of those heroes, do you really think any of us will be able to tackle this alone? So, if we don't work together, we've got no chance of saving our friends and putting a stop to whatever evil is going on over there."

"Well," Mom says. "Pipsqueak here may have a point. I was heading to ArmaTech on my own, but maybe that's not such a good idea."

"Same here," Dad says. "Could be a mistake."

"This mission does sound dangerous," Mom says. "Maybe we should team up. Just for this one."

"Perhaps," Dad says. "If Sunbolt took down powerful heroes like Master Mime and Blue Bolt, it probably makes sense to go together. But just this once."

They look at each other, and then at me.

"Wait," I say. "So, we're really doing this? Like, together?"

"Yes," Dad says. "We'll tackle this mystery together. And we'll see how it goes."

"Exactly," Mom says.

"Yes!" I say. "I mean, great. Let's do this."

***

Fifteen minutes later I'm back in the woods outside of ArmaTech. But this time I'm not alone. Mom, Dad, and Gigi are with me, and they're ready for action.

"Okay," Mom says. "Where was this secret entrance you were talking about?"

"Over there," I say, pointing to the west side of the building. "It leads right into the laboratory. It's going to be a tight squeeze, but once we're inside we should pop out across from the alien captive. Are you guys ready?"

But instead of response, I get silence.

"What?" I ask.

"Did you just say 'alien' captive?" Dad asks.

"You never said anything about an alien captive," Mom says.

"Oh, well, I guess I forgot that part," I say, blushing beneath my helmet. I guess some things never change, even when you're being grilled by young adult versions of your parents.

"Do you want to fill us in?" Dad asks. "You know, before we risk our lives raiding the place."

"Um, sure," I say. "Well, when I was inside, I discovered an alien guy named Proog who was being held prisoner. Apparently, he's part of some kind of space police force called the Intergalactic Paladins. He came to Earth to hide something called the Cosmic Key which is the only thing keeping an extraterrestrial bad guy named Krule the Conqueror locked in the 13th Dimension. But before he could leave Earth, Proog was ambushed by Sunbolt and Norman Fairchild, the owner of ArmaTech, who are searching for the Cosmic Key for some reason. Does that make sense?"

But they don't answer. They just stare at me.

"Sooo," Mom says, finally breaking the silence, "somehow you forgot to tell us all of that?"

"Um, yeah," I say. "Sorry, there's a lot going on."

"Is there anything else in there you'd like to share?" Dad asks. "You know, just out of curiosity? Santa Claus? Big Foot? A unicorn? Anything?"

Well, there's like, millions of things, but I can't tell them that.

"Nope," I say. "I think we're all good now."

"Swell," Dad says. "Well, I've never seen an alien before. So, this should be… educational."

"I'm with you on that one," Mom says.

Wait, what? In my timestream, my parents have dealt with all sorts of aliens! My mind races through all the extraterrestrial races I've encountered: the Skelton, the Dhoom, my friends on the Zodiac. So how is it that these two have never seen an alien?

Then, I remember how young they are. I mean, they haven't even formed the Freedom Force yet. So, I guess it makes sense.

"Okay," Dad says. "Enough talking. Let's get in there and do some damage."

"Whoa, slow down, cowboy," Mom says. "Let's take it nice and easy."

"Great idea," Dad says. "How about we knock on the front door?"

Oh no. Here they go again. I'm about to interject when Dad says, "Um, where's your dog going?"

My heart stops as I look over to find Gigi headed straight for ArmaTech! What's she doing? Then, she turns invisible.

Well, she'll make it undetected, but how will the rest of us… OMG! I'm such a nitwit sometimes.

I concentrate hard, pushing my Meta Manipulation powers towards Gigi's location. Then, I pull them back, capturing her power of invisibility.

Then, I turn it on.

"Hey," Dad says, "where'd you go?"

"I'm still here," I say. "I'm invisible, just like you."

I reach out and grab my parents' arms.

"Where'd Brainstorm go?" Dad says.

"I can't see you either, genius," Mom says.

"Stay calm," I say. "We're all invisible now. Just don't let go of me."

"How'd you do that?" Dad asks.

"Long story," I say. "But now we can get inside without being seen. So, grab my hand. I'm not sure if I can keep this up if we're not connected."

They each grab one of my hands.

"Ready?" I ask.

"It's Fight Time!" Dad says.

"Seriously?" Mom says.

But I don't wait for Dad's response. Instead, I take off with my parents in tow. As we bolt across the terrain towards ArmaTech, I'm smiling the whole way. I'd like to say it's because we're about to solve this mystery. But I know it's because I've been homesick for so long that it feels great to have my parents with me, even if they're barely older than Grace.

A minute later, we reach the hidden entrance. I whisper Gigi's name, but she doesn't respond.

"Your dog is super annoying," Dad whispers.

"Well," I say, "she's not really my—"

"Shhh," Mom whispers. "I can sense our friends are

inside, but I'm only getting faint readings. We should move before someone realizes we're out here."

"Okay," I say, "follow me."

I drop to my hands and knees and lead them through the opening. When we pop out the other side, I whisper Gigi's name again but there's still nothing. I scan the room. All of the other animals are here, but not her.

Then, I look up and my stomach sinks.

Proog's cell is empty.

Where is he?

I feel Dad's hand on my back.

"What's all this for?" he whispers.

"It's an animal testing center," I whisper back.

"That's horrible," Mom whispers.

"So, where's the alien?" Dad whispers.

"I… I don't know," I whisper back. "He was right there, in that cell. But he's gone." I try sounding calm, but deep inside I'm panicking. I mean, what happened to Proog? Did they move him? Or… worse?

"I sense our friends are close," Mom whispers. "They're down that hallway."

That's the corridor I came through the first time. It leads to that other passageway I didn't take. The one that ran right instead of left.

"Stay connected," I say. "And follow me."

Mom puts her hand on my shoulder and we move, running single file, down the stark white corridor. While my eyes are looking straight ahead, my mind is elsewhere.

I mean, I shouldn't have listened to Proog. I should have saved him while I could. But instead, I took off like a coward.

And now it's too late.

We approach the intersection.

"Stay straight," Mom whispers.

I follow her instructions and head down the hallway. This one is just as white as the others, but for some reason it feels like it's narrowing with every step. Of course, at this point I'm so distraught my mind could be playing tricks on me.

Then, everything opens up and I stop short.

Mom crashes into me, and Dad into her.

No one says a word.

That's because we're standing in an unusual room. The space is cavernous, with a ceiling that looks a hundred feet high and walls that are smooth and curved. But the shape of the room is not what has us speechless.

Along the walls are dozens of glass-domed pods, each one perfectly equidistant from the next. And they're all connected to a grid of metal pipes that seems to be running towards a central location—a sealed, metal chamber with a chair in the center.

What's that for?

"Look!" Mom whispers, pointing up high.

I glance up and squint, and to my surprise I find a face staring right back at me! It's the face of a masked girl with pigtails!

It's… it's… Sunbolt?

But how could she be up there?

Then, I scan the other pods and find more faces.

It's the heroes!

They're inside the pods!

What's going on?

I'm about to ask my parents, when I realize I can see them. Which means my invisibility powers have worn off!

"Uh oh," Dad says, looking at us. "What happened?"

I have no idea.

"Welcome…" comes a deep, familiar voice.

We spin around to find a large frame filling the corridor, blocking our exit.

It's Fairchild!

And he's huge! In fact, he's so huge I don't think I realized how huge he was when I saw him in the lab. He's wearing a suit and a tie, and for some reason the only thing on my mind is where he got a suit that big.

"… and good night," he continues, waving something in the air that looks like a stick.

Then, it glows orange.

And I'm out.

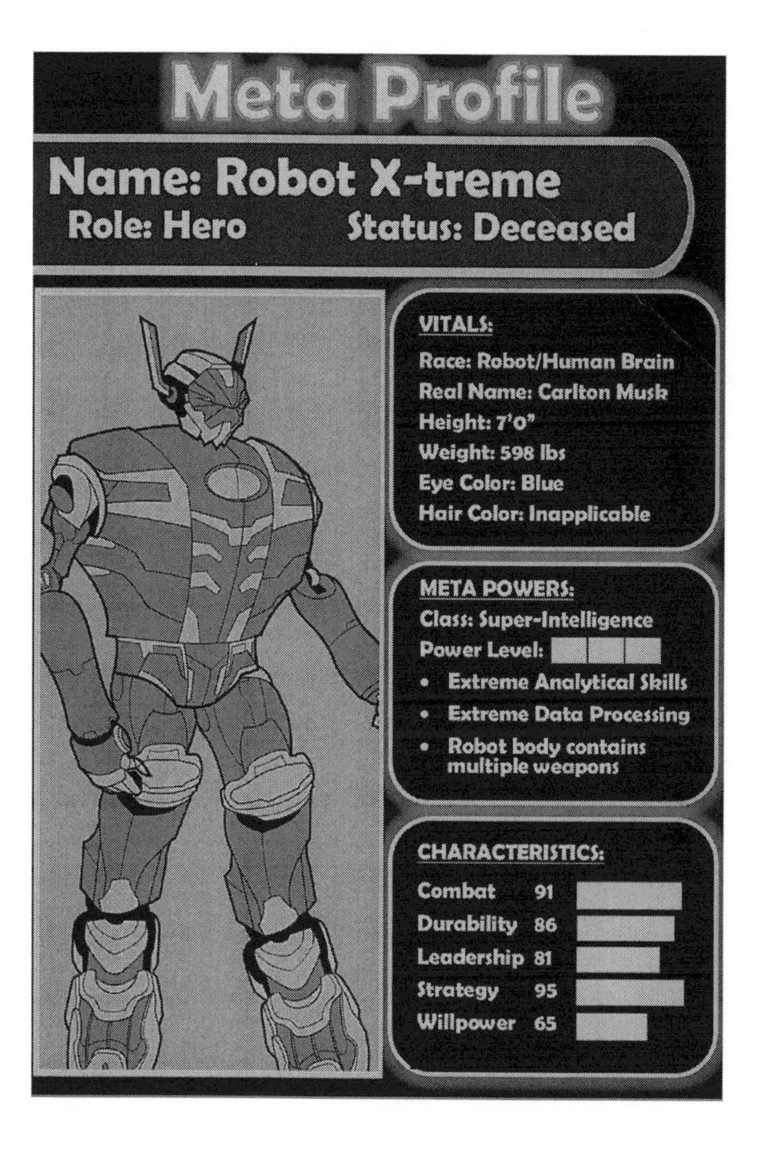
Meta Profile
Name: Robot X-treme
Role: Hero
Status: Deceased
VITALS:
Race: Robot/Human Brain
Real Name: Carlton Musk
Height: 7'0"
Weight: 598 lbs
Eye Color: Blue
Hair Color: Inapplicable
META POWERS:
Class: Super-Intelligence
Power Level:
• Extreme Analytical Skills
• Extreme Data Processing
• Robot body contains multiple weapons
CHARACTERISTICS:
Combat 91
Durability 86
Leadership 81
Strategy 95
Willpower 65

TWELVE

I FLUNK MY INTERVIEW

As soon as I open my eyes, I know I'm in trouble.

I'm lying on my back, staring at a bright, white ceiling. To my sides are cages, and by my feet is a cart filled with surgical instruments. I don't need Super-Intelligence to know where I am.

The animal testing lab!

I try sitting up, but my arms and legs are strapped to a table, and my helmet is so heavy I can barely lift my head. But from what I can gather, other than the lab animals, there's no one here but me.

Where are my parents?

I flex my muscles, but the straps hold firm. It's no use, I'm tied down tight. This is not good.

I don't know what I'm doing here, but I certainly

don't plan on staying long. After all, I don't want to end up like these poor animals. I've got to get out of here, and fast, before—

"Excellent," comes a deep voice. "You're awake."

—that.

Suddenly, a man's face appears overhead, startling me. He has dark brown hair and crystal blue eyes. I know him immediately.

"F-Fairchild!" I stutter.

"Yes," he says. "I'm flattered you know me, but unfortunately, I don't know you. And that doesn't seem fair, does it? So, tell me, who are you and what are you doing here?"

I don't know what to say. I'm certainly not going to tell him my real name or that I'm from the future.

"None of your business," I snap.

"Perhaps I should warn you that now isn't the time for games," he says, grinning ear to ear. "Because when I play games, I never lose. Now, let's try this one more time. Who are you and what are you doing here?"

"Where's Liberty Lad and Brainstorm?" I demand.

"Enjoying a deep sleep," he says. "Like the others."

"What are you doing to them?" I ask. "Why are you capturing all of these heroes?"

"That's simple," he says. "They are subjects for an experiment I'm conducting."

Experiment?

"What kind of experiment?" I ask.

"An experiment in power," he says. "Which is why I find you so interesting. You seem to possess a lot of power, don't you?"

Huh? How does he know I have powers?

"I'm not telling you anything," I say.

"You won't have to," he says. "Not while I have this."

Then, he waves a long, thin object in front of my face. At first, it looks like a silver baton. But upon closer inspection, I see white dots twinkling inside, like… stars?

Then it hits me.

I know exactly what that is.

"The Infinity Wand!" I say.

"Ah, I see you've heard of it," he says, staring into it. "It's a fascinating object, isn't it? I thought they were just a myth, but when I learned they were real I had to have one for myself. They're quite powerful. I believe they detect and amplify Meta energy, just like this."

He tilts the Infinity Wand over my head and an orange spark flashes out the end.

"I imagine that in the right hands," he continues, "it would be quite a powerful weapon."

"That's Proog's!" I yell. "Where is he?"

"Proog?" he says, furrowing his brow. "Oh, yes. Proog. Was that the name of the alien? Well, unfortunately, he expired. I guess his heart was not as strong as his resolve."

"Wait," I say. "Y-You mean, he's dead?" I ask.

"Oh, yes," Fairchild says, waving the wand. "Very dead indeed. But don't worry, I'll take good care of his toy."

"You don't deserve that!" I yell. "Proog was a hero!"

"He was, wasn't he?" Fairchild says. "But he's gone now. So, I guess I'll have to stand in for him. Fortunately, I won't be distracted by any pointless hero obligations."

This guy is nuts! But I can't break free.

"By the way," he continues. "I must thank you for completing my hero collection. I knew if I let you escape, you would come back with others in tow. And that's exactly what you did."

What's he talking about? And then, my blood runs cold. He knew I was watching him with Proog!

"Y-You mean, you knew I was there? And you just let me go?"

"Of course, I knew you were there," he says. "The Infinity Wand told me so."

I feel like such a heel. I mean, I led my parents right into his trap! Some son I am.

"I may not be a hero," he continues, "but I'm certainly no fool. So, let's get back to you, shall we? Tell me, who are you?"

But I clam up.

"I completely understand if you don't want to volunteer information," he says, moving out of view. "But by now I hope you realize I will get to the truth… one way or another."

I hear CLINKING noises by my feet. I look out of the corner of my eye and see him by the surgical cart. What's he doing? Then, he lifts a syringe into the air!

He's going to stick me with something!

I try busting out again, but I can't.

Suddenly, he appears overhead again, syringe in hand!

"Shall we begin?" he asks.

RUFF!

Fairchild turns.

What's that? It sounded like it came from far away.

RUFF! RUFF!

That's a dog barking!

Gigi! And she sounds really upset.

Fairchild puts down the syringe.

"Excuse me," he says. "It appears one of my specimens escaped from its cage. We'll continue later."

Then, he disappears, his footsteps echoing down the hall. Relief washes over me. Man, Gigi is the best. I just hope she disappears before Fairchild shows up. Now I've got to get out of here, before it's too late. But how?

"Shhh!" comes a voice to my left.

I jump out of my skin.

"Relax" a man says. "I'm going to free you."

Then, a masked face appears overhead.

But it's not just any mask, it's a… hawk mask?

"Shadow Hawk?" I say.

"Shhh!" he whispers. "Quiet, kid. Let's get you out of here."

I hear RIPPING, and suddenly my arms and legs are free! They feel totally numb, so I shake them out to get some circulation going. But even though I can barely feel my limbs, my heart is pumping fast with excitement, because standing before me is one of the greatest heroes of all time. Except, he's unusually thin.

Then, I remember I'm back in the past. So, this skinny guy is a younger version of Shadow Hawk!

"How did you find me?" I ask.

"I wasn't looking for you, kid," he says, folding his hawk-knife and placing it into his utility belt. "I was looking for the Gray Ghost."

"The Gray Ghost?" I say, totally confused. Who's that? Then, everything clicks. The Gray Ghost. GG. Those were the initials on Gigi's tag! "Hang on, you mean the dog is a superhero? The invisible dog, right?"

"That's the one," Shadow Hawk says, helping me to my feet. "And believe me, keeping tabs on her isn't easy."

"So I've heard," I say. "But why are you following her?"

"Because she's Sunbolt's dog," Shadow Hawk says. "Before Blue Bolt and Master Mime disappeared, they told me they were working with Sunbolt. Since then, all sorts of heroes have vanished. Yet, Sunbolt's still around. So, I got suspicious. Clearly, she's up to no good."

"You've got that right," I say. "Sunbolt is the Trickster."

"Yeah," he says. "I figured. The problem is that I've

had a hard time tracking her down. Then, I found her dog running loose around Keystone City. So, I put a homing device inside a piece of bread, hoping she'd bite, and she did. But she never led me to Sunbolt. That is, until she teamed up with you. So, that's how I got here. Now I haven't seen you around before, but I figured anyone Fairchild's tied to a table has to be one of the good guys. What's your story?"

I desperately want to tell him, but I can't.

"I'm the Nullifier," I say. "I… sort of got swept up into this mess."

"Pleased to meet you, Nullifier," Shadow Hawk says, shaking my hand. "But I hope you're ready, because this mess is only going to get messier."

"Yeah, I'm sure," I say. "Listen, our friends are stuck in these strange pods in the other room, but I've got no clue why. And now Fairchild has the Infinity Wand."

"Yes," Shadow Hawk says. "I heard him talking about it, although I'm not sure what it does. But it belonged to a friend of yours, huh?"

"Proog," I say. "I can't say we were friends, but we certainly felt like kindred spirits. And based on what Fairchild did to him, we're going to have to move fast to save the others."

"I'm with you," Shadow Hawk says. "Let's end this."

But just as we're about to get going, my eyes fall on the rat cage. It seems like there are hundreds of them in there, milling about, stepping all over one another.

But then something odd catches my eye.

At the top of the pile is a teeny, tiny rat.

He's clearly the runt of the litter, yet he's super determined, fighting to stay on top of the pack. As he balances precariously on top of another rat's head, his paws are flailing, like he's waving at me.

"Hang on," I say.

"Now may not be the best time to pet the animals," Shadow Hawk says.

But I scoop up the little rat anyway. He fits perfectly in my palm. Strangely, he's not putting up a fight. In fact, he looks like he wants to be held. What gives?

But then, my eyes land on the surgical cart. There's a bunch of syringes laid out, including one labeled: *Truth Serum*. Well, I guess Fairchild was going to use that one on me.

But then I see a syringe marked: *Brain Growth Serum #2324*. That's weird, why does that number seem so familiar?

Then, I look at the rat's tag. It reads: *#2324B*.

B? For Brain Growth Serum?

Suddenly, a particular Meta profile springs to mind, and I look into the little rat's pink eyes.

O. M. G!

This is no run-of-the-mill rat!

It's baby TechnocRat!

Meta Profile
Name: Gray Ghost
Role: Hero
Status: Deceased
VITALS:
Race: German Shepherd
Real Name: Gray Ghost
Height: 2'0" (at shoulder)
Weight: 81 lbs
Eye Color: Dark Brown
Hair Color: Gray/Black
META POWERS:
Class: Meta-Morph
Power Level:
• Considerable Invisibility
• Can turn all or part of body invisible
CHARACTERISTICS:
Combat 54
Durability 14
Leadership 20
Strategy 18
Willpower 70

THIRTEEN

I SEEM TO ATTRACT BAD NEWS

I think my ears are gonna fall off.

Ever since we injected the Brain Growth Serum into that tiny rat, he's been talking a mile a minute. But I guess I shouldn't be surprised, after all, we've just created TechnocRat.

"—about time," he says. "I've been cooped up in that cage with those squeakers for way too long. Do you have any clue what they blabber about all day? Cheese! All day it's 'cheese this,' and 'cheese that,' and 'where's the cheese?' There are one hundred and seventy-three rats in that box and not a single one has an original thought. Trust me, after about two seconds you'd want to—"

"Does he ever shut up?" Shadow Hawk asks.

"Do you really want the answer?" I respond.

"—and here's another problem—," TechnocRat

drones on.

Then, a strange thought crosses my mind. I mean, I knew TechnocRat came from ArmaTech, but I never thought I'd be the one bringing him to life! Maybe I was too impulsive, but the syringe was sitting right there. If I didn't do it, who knows if Fairchild would have ever gotten to it. I mean, this timestream is screwy enough.

Well, I certainly can't take it back now. What's done is done. I just hope creating TechnocRat hasn't destroyed my future. Or my hearing.

"—and rats just don't work well together. Never have, never will. I told those bozos that if we got on the same page, we could open the cage ourselves. But you know what they said? 'Where's the cheese?' I'll tell you, they have the collective intelligence of a rock. In fact—"

I can't take it.

"—don't think they could find their way out of a maze if they were given a map. In fact, I'm going to give them a map and—"

"Quiet!" I blurt out, covering his tiny mouth with my index finger. "Please, can we just have some peace and quiet for a second?"

"Mmmmkay," he mumbles, looking at me with his wide, beady eyes.

I'm about to start talking but stop myself. I need to be careful. I can't tell him too much, otherwise I may compromise the timestream. I'll have to choose my words carefully and only tell him what he needs to know.

"Listen, we need your help," I say. "You may not know it yet, but you're the smartest creature on the planet. In fact, you're a Meta hero, a big-time hero, and we need your help to save a bunch of other heroes who are in trouble. Capeesh?"

TechnocRat nods slowly.

"Great," I say, removing my finger. "So, let's stop talking about cheese, and let's focus on what needs to be done right now. Are you with us?"

"Completely," TechnocRat says, sniffing the air. "But before we save the world, I've got two questions."

"Shoot," I say.

"First, who the heck are you and what's with the scary guy with the beak?"

"I'm the Nullifier," I say, "and that's Shadow Hawk. We're the good guys."

"Got it," he says, his ears perking up. "So, if I'm a hero, I need a superhero name, too! Like…" then he strikes a pose, raising his claws over his head, "… Attack Rat!"

"How about ir-RAT-ating?" Shadow Hawk says. "Can we go now?"

"Hang on," I say. "What was your second question?"

"Oh, yeah," TechnocRat says. "Why is your finger fading in and out like that?"

My finger? What's he talking about? But when I look down, I see that he's right! My finger is pulsating—from solid to see-through and then back again! What's going on? I mean, I lost Gigi's invisibility power a while ago.

Then it hits me.

O.M.G.

I'm… disappearing from existence!

If I don't solve this, it'll be the end of me.

"You okay?" Shadow Hawk asks.

"Yeah," I say, lying. "I-I'm fine. Let's get moving."

Shadow Hawk nods and takes off. I cup TechnocRat in my hands and follow.

"How about 'IncinerRat?'" TechnocRat rambles on. "Or 'ObliteRat'. Or 'The PiRat King?'"

But I've got so many things running through my brain I can't even respond. I run down the list. Fairchild has captured my parents and the others for some kind of experiment. Sunbolt is the Trickster, but she's in one of the pods too. So, how's that possible? Proog is dead, and Fairchild has his Infinity Wand, which probably isn't good news. I haven't heard Gigi bark in a while. And there's been no sign of the Time Trotter anywhere.

Oh, and to top it off, I'm fading into nothingness.

It's been a great day.

Then, I look down and nearly faint.

Now the top of my left hand is transparent!

It's spreading!

If I don't figure this out fast, I'm toast!

Thankfully, I've got Shadow Hawk with me, one of the greatest heroes of all time. And now we've got TechnocRat, the greatest brain on the planet.

"How about… 'The eRaticator?'" TechnocRat asks.

Although you wouldn't know it by listening to him.

But if anyone can figure out this mess, it'll be him.

I hope.

We charge down the hallway, passing the intersection. To say I have a bad feeling about this is an understatement. But there's no turning back now. It doesn't help that it's nearly impossible to breathe through this helmet. I want to just rip it off, but I can't let them see my face. It's too risky, even though it feels like I'm going to hyperventilate.

Suddenly, the space opens up and we skid to a halt.

We're inside Fairchild's chamber!

I scan the circular room to find all of the pods still in place. Then, I look to my left and find two pods occupied with new faces. It's Mom and Dad!

Then, I look up.

It's Sunbolt! She's still inside!

"Whoa," TechnocRat says, pointing straight ahead. "Look at that guy."

It's Fairchild! He's sealed inside the chamber, wearing a helmet and harness connected to a mess of wires. What's he doing?

"Allow me," Shadow Hawk says, pulling out a Hawk-a-rang.

But as soon as he throws it, it's engulfed in flames and disintegrates before our eyes. What gives?

"Sorry," comes a girl's voice. "But this isn't a fire-free zone."

I turn, and my jaw hits the floor.

It's Sunbolt!

I look up again, and there she is, unconscious inside her pod. But when I look back down, she's standing right in front of us. That's just not possible.

Unless.

Unless…

Oh, no.

I think I'm gonna hurl.

"Move it!" TechnocRat yells, leaping out of my hands.

I hear his voice, but I don't react. I'm staring at Sunbolt, but my brain is a step behind. It's not until my eyes focus that I realize her hands are pointed right at me.

Uh-oh.

Fire blazes from her fingertips.

I can't react!

But before it hits me, I'm bowled over.

FWOOSH!

There's a huge explosion, followed by an ear-piercing YELP!

I'm lying on the ground stunned, but when I sit up Gigi materializes out of thin air. She's lying beside me, the fur on her back singed black. She saved me!

"Gigi!" I yell.

I put my hand on her stomach. She's still breathing, thank goodness. But she's hurt. I can see large blisters forming on her back. She needs medical attention.

"Well, at least I got that annoying dog," Sunbolt says. "She wouldn't leave me alone."

"That's because she knows you're a fraud!" I yell.

"I am?" Sunbolt says. Then she wheels around and fires a blast at Shadow Hawk, who barely somersaults out of the way. "You don't know anything about me."

"Not true!" I yell. "I know exactly who you are!"

I focus my negation powers, and then push them towards Sunbolt. Suddenly, she begins to flicker, and then her body begins to morph into something else.

Something big and muscular.

And my greatest fear is realized.

"Holy guacamole," TechnocRat whispers.

"What is that?" Shadow Hawk asks, alarmed.

In Sunbolt's place stands a yellow-skinned, pointy-eared creature—staring me down with neon green eyes.

"That is a Blood Bringer," I say.

"And what is a Blood Bringer?" TechnocRat asks.

"An elite warrior from a bloodthirsty race of alien shape-shifters known as the Skelton," I answer.

"Well, that's disturbing," TechnocRat says.

But my back tenses up, because I know this is no ordinary Blood Bringer. All of the other Blood Bringers I've seen can transform into an unlimited number of forms. But this Blood Bringer is different. This one not only copied Sunbolt's form, but also her Energy Manipulation powers.

"Who are you?" I ask.

"My true name is inconsequential," he says. "But I am impressed, for it seems you do know of me. Or, at least, my kind. But you demean me by calling me a mere Blood Bringer, for I am so much more than that. Within the Skelton Empire, I am known as the Blood Master. Now prepare to die!"

But as he tries to power up, nothing happens.

"What have you done?" the Blood Master demands. "I cannot activate my powers."

"Sorry about that," I say. "Well, not really."

"No matter," the Skelton says, pulling a long sword from behind his back. "I won't need powers to destroy the likes of you." Then, he twirls the sword effortlessly, like he's starring in a karate movie.

I swallow hard. He's probably right.

Suddenly, there's a blinding FLASH of white light.

I block my eyes, but not in time.

Where'd that come from?

But as my vision returns, I realize the light is coming from Fairchild's chamber. I shield my eyes, and squint in his direction. And that's when I see it.

Held high in Fairchild's hands.

The Infinity Wand!

"Stop them!" Fairchild barks. "I must concentrate. Don't let them interfere with my experiment."

"Experiment?" the Blood Master scoffs. "This is no experiment, fool. The fate of the universe is in our hands!"

"Yes," Fairchild says. "But it will all have been for nothing if I fail."

"Failure is not an option," the Blood Master says. "Now get on with it. I'll handle these vermin."

"Um, did he just call me vermin?" TechnocRat says. "Because I've never been so insulted in my life."

With sword in hand, the Blood Master lunges at Shadow Hawk, who dodges it with ease. But I don't know how long this can last. I mean, Shadow Hawk is an amazing fighter, but the Skelton are ruthless.

Then, Fairchild pulls a lever inside his chamber, and all of the pods radiate with orange energy.

"What's going on?" I ask.

But before anyone can answer, the orange energy transfers from the pods to the metal pipes, and then runs towards Fairchild's chamber.

"Based on what I'm seeing," TechnocRat says, "I'd say he's built a Meta conductor."

"A Meta what?" I say.

"A Meta conductor," TechnocRat says. "Typically, conductors are used to transfer electrical currents. But this one looks like it's designed to transfer Meta energy. What I haven't figured out yet is how he's actually pulling the Meta energy out of the hero's bodies."

Great, if he can't figure it out, we're doomed.

I look back at Fairchild to find the orange energy crackling around his helmet and harness. Then, he lifts the Infinity Wand higher, and the intergalactic weapon releases a huge burst of orange energy! It whips around the room, shattering everything it touches! Shadow Hawk and the Blood Master duck beneath a tentacle, which lashes into the wall behind them.

This is nuts! The Meta energy is destroying everything it touches! We've got to stop it before it wipes us out! And the heroes stuck in their pods are helpless!

But before I can react, the wild energy is suddenly sucked back over Fairchild's chamber, forming a giant orange ball.

What's happening?

I look at Fairchild's sweaty face. He's concentrating hard. It looks like he's focusing, trying to control it!

Then, the ball loses its shape.

It's too strong!

But to my surprise, it reforms, and then morphs into a giant, upside down 'U.'

"What's he doing now?" I ask.

"No clue," TechnocRat says.

Suddenly, the ground RUMBLES beneath us, sending us flying like popcorn kernels. I land hard on my backside. That's gonna leave a bruise.

But as I look back, the ground beneath the orange 'U' has completely separated. Debris is spewing up everywhere. It's like he's created some kind of a giant vacuum cleaner, sucking up the earth below!

But why would he do that?

Then, I remember Proog's words: "*We believed if we buried it here, it would stay here instead of drifting aimlessly through space where it could fall into the wrong hands.*"

Buried?

O.M.G!

"I know what he's doing!" I say. "He's using the Infinity Wand to create a Meta magnet! He's—"

BOOM!

There's a massive explosion, and suddenly I'm flying through the air. I hit the wall hard, followed by TechnocRat who slams into my stomach. Then, we drop to the floor.

I pick myself up, but it feels like I've been run over by a truck. I have a funny feeling this is far from over.

And when I look up, I know I'm right.

Because attached to the bottom of Fairchild's Meta magnet is a strange purple object.

But it's no ordinary object.

It's the Cosmic Key!

Meta Profile
Name: Blood Master
Role: Villain Status: Active
VITALS:
Race: Skelton
Real Name: Unknown
Height: 6'11"
Weight: 330 lbs
Eye Color: Green
Hair Color: Bald
META POWERS:
Class: Meta-morph
Power Level:
• Extreme Shape-Shifting—can assume endless forms
• Can mimic the powers of those he assumes the form of
CHARACTERISTICS:
Combat 100
Durability 91
Leadership 85
Strategy 88
Willpower 92

FOURTEEN

I FUMBLE THE KEY TO SUCCESS

I can't believe it.

I'm staring at the freaking Cosmic Key!

My first thought is that it's way bigger than I imagined. In fact, it looks like one of those giant 'keys-to-the-city' keys you always see the mayor handing out on the six o'clock news. Except this one is deep purple and has a strangely celestial glow around it.

My second thought is that I'm pretty sure this key is much more than just a key. I mean, the Orb of Oblivion was a living entity that fed off of the desires of its host. I still shudder just thinking about it! Plus, it took absolutely forever to get that thing out of my life.

So, my instincts are telling me to stay as far away from that key as possible.

But my gut is telling me that ain't gonna happen.

After all, I can't just sit here and watch it fall into the wrong hands. According to Proog, the Cosmic Key is the only thing keeping Krule the Conqueror and his band of bad guys prisoner in the 13th Dimension. I'd love to stay on the sidelines, but if they ended up terrorizing the universe, I couldn't forgive myself.

So, I've got to do something.

But what?

Both Fairchild and the Blood Master seem to have forgotten all about us. They're totally fixated on the Cosmic Key. It's like they're stranded on a desert island and the Cosmic Key is the only piece of food around.

One thing I still don't understand is why Fairchild has partnered with the Skelton? Doesn't he realize how dangerous they are? Or is something else going on here?

"Finally!" the Blood Master exclaims. "The Cosmic Key is mine! With Krule's only means of escape from the 13th Dimension in my possession, there will be no one left to challenge the Skelton Empire! We will rule the universe unopposed!"

"Will you?" Fairchild says matter-of-factly. "Because I don't remember agreeing to that."

"You?" the Blood Master says. "What are you talking about? We had a deal, human. I brought you an Infinity Wand, and you were to deliver me the Cosmic Key."

"Yes, and thank you," Fairchild says looking at his Infinity Wand. "But perhaps you misheard me. I said I would deliver the Cosmic Key. But I never said I'd give it to you."

"Traitor!" the Blood Master screams, pointing his sword at Fairchild. "We promised you Earth in exchange for the Cosmic Key. If you renege on our deal, we will destroy you and your pathetic planet."

"Tell me, Skelton filth," Fairchild says. "Why would anyone settle for Earth, when they could rule the universe?"

"Filth?" the Blood Master says, his eyes wild. "You will regret that remark."

"Um, guys," I whisper to TechnocRat and Shadow Hawk. "I think now would be a good time to free the heroes. Because this is about to get ugly. Like, really ugly."

They nod and move to opposite sides of the room.

I'd love to help them, but something tells me to hold my spot. I mean, I'm still negating the Blood Master's powers, and that's important, but for some reason I can't take my eyes off the Cosmic Key.

It's mesmerizing.

"You will pay for your disloyalty," the Blood Master spits, holding out his sword. Then, he charges Fairchild, yelling, "Prepare to die!"

But Fairchild simply smiles and says, "You first."

There's an earsplitting KRAKOW as a tremendous bolt of orange energy splinters from Fairchild's Meta magnet, and I'm blown backwards by its enormous force.

I slam into the wall behind me, and for a second, I'm

seeing stars. But as my eyesight returns, I realize my head feels lighter. That's when I reach up and realize my helmet is gone! It's been blown to smithereens!

But that's not the biggest surprise.

When I look over at the Blood Master, he's lying face-down, his body smoldering with orange smoke.

That Meta blast totally leveled him.

He… he isn't moving!

"Fool!" Fairchild crows victorious.

Suddenly, I feel guilty. I mean, I essentially made the Blood Master defenseless against Fairchild. But maybe I made a huge mistake? What if Fairchild is actually the greater evil?

"You okay, dude?" comes a familiar voice.

I turn to find Dad standing next to me!

He's free! But he looks totally confused.

Then, other heroes start dropping from the ceiling.

Rolling Thunder! Madame Meteorite! Blue Bolt! Dynamo Joe! Master Mime! Robot X-treme!

Shadow Hawk and TechnocRat did it!

They freed the heroes!

But they all look pretty dazed. I guess being stuck in those pods for so long really affected them.

"Ghostie!" comes a girl's voice.

I turn to find Sunbolt running towards Gigi.

"What happened, girl?" she asks, dropping to her knees. "You poor thing!"

Now that's the Sunbolt I remember!

I'm so relieved they're all free.

Except, someone's missing. Where's…

"Hey," comes a female voice.

I feel a hand on my shoulder, and when I turn my eyes meet Mom's.

Her eyebrows go up.

Oh no! Without my helmet, she recognizes me!

"Hey!" she says. "Aren't you that kid those thugs held hostage? And you knew my secret identity. But… but how?"

I lower my eyes. I don't know what to tell her. I mean, how can I possibly explain any of this?

But when I look back up, her face says it all.

She knows everything!

Oh no! With all of the chaos going on, I let my guard down. I forgot to shield my mind from her!

"Y-You're… my… my…," she stutters.

"Please," I say. "You can't tell anyone. You shouldn't know any of this. It might destroy everything."

"With… with… him?" she says, looking at Dad, who's busy brushing pieces of debris out of his long tresses. "I think I'm going to be sick."

"Trust me," I say. "He's not so bad. Give him a chance."

"What's happening to you?" she says, her eyes bulging wide. "You're… you're vanishing."

What? I look down to see my green boots disappearing and reappearing again. Oh jeez!

"You shouldn't be here," she says. "You need to get back to your timestream."

"Yeah," I say. "That's what I've been trying to do. Except I can't. I-I think I'm supposed to be here for some reason. I just don't know what."

"Come back!" Fairchild calls out, snapping me back to reality.

As I look over, I'm shocked. The Cosmic Key is drifting away from Fairchild's Meta magnet. And it's heading straight for the fallen Blood Master!

And Fairchild's Meta magnet looks like it's shrinking!

What's going on?

And then I remember Proog's words.

"The Cosmic Key cannot be contained. It is attracted to Meta energy."

That's it!

The Cosmic Key is attracted to Meta energy.

Fairchild's blast must have transferred so much Meta energy when it zapped the Blood Master that the Cosmic Key is following it.

"Get back here!" Fairchild demands. Desperately, he pulls the lever inside his chamber once again, but then he realizes the pods holding the heroes are empty. There's no Meta energy left for him to siphon.

But Fairchild doesn't stop.

He throws off his helmet and harness and points the Infinity Wand at the Cosmic Key. Suddenly, a huge blast of Meta energy explodes from the Infinity Wand, engulfing the Cosmic Key.

The cosmic entity stops in mid-air.

O.M.G!

The Infinity Wand amplifies Meta energy!

And he's using it to pull back the Cosmic Key!

"We've got to stop him!" Dad declares.

"We're in," Dynamo Joe says.

But just as the heroes unite, there's a loud BOOM, followed by a swirling green vortex—a vortex I know all too well. And when it disappears, it leaves behind two giant figures.

"Um, are those T. Rex?" TechnocRat says.

Are you kidding me right now?

At first, the behemoths look confused. Then, they get their bearings and realize there's plenty of appetizers all around them. They ROAR.

"We'll need to work as a team," Blue Bolt says.

"If we're going to be a team, we need a catchy name," Rolling Thunder says. "How about… the Freedom Force!"

"Surprisingly, I like it," Dad says.

"Thanks," Rolling Thunder says. "Although I feel like I've heard it before."

Well, I guess I won't be getting credit for that one, but that's the least of my problems. Because as the heroes engage the giant lizards, it dawns on me that if dinosaurs are here, the Time Trotter can't be far behind!

But where is he?

Then, I realize Fairchild nearly has the Cosmic Key.

I can't let that happen.

Fortunately, Fairchild isn't the only one who can manipulate Meta energy.

I focus on the Blood Master, who's body is still crackling with Meta energy. I concentrate hard, and then draw all of that energy towards me.

It hits me with a wallop—like a massive power surge.

My body feels electric. Super-charged.

Here goes nothing. I turn towards the Cosmic Key, and open my arms, emitting Meta energy all around me.

The Cosmic Key stops.

Then it heads towards me.

It's working!

I'm pulling it away from Fairchild!

But Fairchild doesn't give up. He pulls harder, and it's like we're playing a game of tug-of-war, with the Cosmic Key in the middle!

"You are powerful, child," Fairchild says. "But not powerful enough."

Then, he points the Infinity Wand at the heroes.

Uh-oh.

Suddenly, a huge blast of orange energy explodes from the wand's tip, heading for a group of the heroes. As the orange wave touches them, they freeze! Then, he pulls their energy back into the Infinity Wand. It's… it's absorbed their powers!

"Now, it ends," Fairchild says, pointing the Infinity

Wand at me! But it's shaking violently—like it's holding too much power.

He's going to obliterate me.

I have seconds to act.

So, I do the first thing that comes to mind.

I gather all of my Meta energy, and push it at the Infinity Wand, sending a giant orange ball straight towards Fairchild.

"NO!" Fairchild yells, his eyes growing wide.

I look for somewhere to hide, but there's no time.

"Duck!" Mom yells, pulling me to the ground.

There's a massive explosion.

Everything goes black for a second, and when I open my eyes, I find myself lying next to Mom.

We made it! But how?

Then, I notice someone is kneeling in front of us.

"You… you blocked the blast," Mom says. "You saved us?"

"Of course," Dad says. "I may be an ignoramus, but I'm an invulnerable ignoramus. Besides, we agreed to team-up for this one, didn't we?"

Mom looks at me and smiles.

"Told ya," I say calmly. But inside I'm bursting at the seams. They're finally getting along! This might actually work out!

"But the dinosaurs took the brunt of it," Dad says.

He's right, because when I look around, the dinosaurs are nowhere to be found. Fortunately, the other heroes seem to be okay. A little worse for wear, but okay.

Poor Fairchild.

I wish I had another option, but he left me with no choice. It was either him or me.

But as the smoke clears, there's a figure still standing.

My jaw drops to the floor.

It's Fairchild!

But… he's even bigger than before.

And his skin and hair are pale white.

Then, he opens his eyes, which blaze with energy.

A familiar orange energy…

Meta Profile
Name: Norman Fairchild
Role: Villain
Status: Deceased
VITALS:
Race: Human
Real Name: Norman Fairchild
Height: 6'6"
Weight: 285 lbs
Eye Color: Brown
Hair Color: Brown
META POWERS:
Class: None
Power Level:
• Meta 0
• Brilliant Scientist
• Founder of ArmaTech Weapons Laboratory
CHARACTERISTICS:
Combat 65
Durability 43
Leadership 28
Strategy 73
Willpower 85

FIFTEEN

I CAN'T BELIEVE WHAT I'VE DONE

I'm speechless.

I close my eyes and then open them again, hoping beyond hope that what I'm seeing isn't real. But unfortunately, everything matches up perfectly. The massive frame. The bone white hair and skin. The wild, orange energy blazing around his eyes.

I'd know him anywhere.

The greatest monster to ever walk the planet.

Meta-Taker.

And he was created by me.

"Who's that?" Dad asks. "And what happened to Fairchild?"

I want to tell Dad that Meta-Taker and Fairchild are one and the same. I want to tell him that I caused the Infinity Wand to explode, infusing Fairchild with its powers. But I just can't form the words. I feel absolutely devastated. I just want to scrunch into a ball and cry.

I mean, is this why I'm here? Was it my destiny to create the most heinous villain in history? Is this how I was supposed to fix the past so I could return to my present? After this, I don't think things can get any worse.

But, surprise, I'm wrong again.

Because when I look at Meta-Taker, I realize he's holding the Cosmic Key.

"Are you okay, Elliott?" Mom whispers.

Hearing her say my real name snaps me back to reality. I desperately want to tell her I'm not okay. In fact, I want to tell her no one here will be okay.

But I can't let her know what happens next. I can't let her know that half of the heroes standing here are about to die. So, I use my Meta powers to shield her from reading my mind.

"Elliott?" she repeats. "Are you blocking me?"

"I'm sorry, Mom," I whisper back. "But there's stuff you just can't know."

To our left, a bunch of the heroes are gathering.

"Let's get that guy!" Rolling Thunder shouts.

"No!" I call out. "You don't understand! He's too dangerous!"

But they don't listen.

Rolling Thunder and Dynamo Joe attack from the sides, but Meta-Taker holds his ground. And then, he uses Master Mime's powers to conjure up a giant purple hammer and clobbers both heroes with one swing.

They CRASH into the wall behind us.

Somebody tugs my arm.

"Eric, what are you doing here?" Sunbolt says, looking at me with a puzzled expression. "You mean, you're a hero? Why didn't you tell me?"

I… I want to answer. But I can't.

"Okay," she says. "We'll deal with that later. But clearly you know this guy. How do we take him down?"

But again, I'm torn. I want to tell her everything, but if I do, it could destroy my timestream.

But if I don't, she'll die.

"And by the way, what's wrong with you?" she says. "You're fading in and out! Is that your power?"

I look down at my body, which is now blinking rapidly like a strobe light! I'm feeling light headed. Is this it? Am I about to disappear from existence?

I look over at Meta-Taker, who's still holding the Cosmic Key in his outstretched hand. The only thing running through my brain is that I'm responsible.

I'm responsible for creating him. I'm responsible for unleashing him on the world. I'm responsible for the deaths of Sunbolt, Dynamo Joe, Rolling Thunder, Madame Meteorite, Robot X-treme, and countless others.

I'm responsible for everything.

But as my eyes fixate on the Cosmic Key, images of other cosmic entities fill my mind.

The Orb of Oblivion.

The Building Block.

The Orb of Oblivion 2.

All of them are gone now. Destroyed.

Blown to pieces.

Blown to…

Then, I get an idea!

If I can blow up the Cosmic Key, I can destroy Meta-Taker before his reign of terror ever begins! I can save my friends and redeem myself! I can erase the mistake I've made!

Even if it costs me my own life.

Suddenly, I have absolute clarity.

I know what I've got to do.

"Get out of here," I yell to the heroes. "All of you!"

"Elliott, wait!" Mom calls out.

But I'm already gone.

I've borrowed Blue Bolt's speed and Dad's strength.

I'm running so fast, everything around me seems like it's moving in slow motion.

I'm five feet away.

I just need to snatch the Cosmic Key and rip it in half. Then, all of this will be over.

Four feet.

I think about Dog-Gone and Grace.

Three feet.

Hopefully, they'll still make it.

Two feet.

Because after this, I'll be finished. But it's worth it.

One foot.

Meta-Taker looks up, his eyes growing wide. I'm nearly on top of him. But as I reach for the Cosmic Key, something huge swoops across my line of sight, taking the key right out of the monster's hand!

No!

I barrel into Meta-Taker and we both go tumbling to the ground. But when I look up, I'm shocked, because there's a Pterodactyl flying through the air—with the Cosmic Key in its mouth!

Then, the prehistoric dinosaur is swallowed up by a green vortex, Cosmic Key and all!

"Finally," comes a booming voice from above.

And that's when I see him, his red, three-eyed head floating above us all. It's him! It's Krule the Conqueror!

"Finally!" Krule says, his voice echoing through the chamber. "The Cosmic Key is mine! And now, the universe will be mine as well!"

Then, there's a huge flash of white light and his image is gone, taking my only chance of destroying Meta-Taker with him.

I'm broken. I don't know what to do next.

But I don't have to wait long for an answer, because I'm suddenly lifted into the air. The next thing I know, I'm face-to-face with Meta-Taker!

All of my nightmares from our first encounter come racing back. The penetrating stare. The rotten breath. The evil grin. I look into his eyes. There's absolutely nothing left of Fairchild in there.

My hatred swells, and I swing at him, but it's no use.

I've expended everything I had.

But then, there's a huge blast of fire, and Meta-Taker ROARS in pain. As he tries to protect himself, he drops me to the ground. But the fire is so intense it pushes him into the wall!

"Hands off my friend, creep!" Sunbolt yells.

I land on my back. I want to stand up, but I can't. My vision is getting blurry, and I-I can't feel my legs!

Suddenly, I hear, "Let me go!"

I look up to find Mom and Gigi standing over me. I'm so happy Gigi's okay. But they're holding someone captive. It's a man, with a green costume and a cone-shaped helmet.

It's the Time Trotter!

"I sensed him lurking in the corner when that flying lizard showed up," Mom says. "So, I took him down with a psychic blast. And then the Gray Ghost pulled this off his wrist."

She holds up a watch.

His time-travelling watch!

Mom kneels over me and puts it in my hand.

"You've got to leave now, Elliott," she whispers urgently. "I looked inside your mind and set the watch to where you need to go."

"No," I say. "I-I have to stop Meta-Taker, you don't understand."

"You're wrong, son," she says, with a sad smile. "I do understand. I'm so proud of you. You're a real hero. But now you have to leave."

Suddenly, there's a loud ROAR!

Meta-Taker!

"N-No," I say, panicked. "I-I can't."

"Elliott," she says. "If you die here, there's no telling what could happen to the future. When I looked into your mind, I saw you save the world—several times over. If you're not there, billions could die. Now listen to me. You must use your powers. You must go now. Trust me, I'll cover your tracks here."

I look into her eyes, and I know she's right.

I've done all I could do here.

This may be my last chance.

I look at Gigi and say, "Bye, girl."

I close my eyes and tap into the watch.

"Goodbye, son," she says. "I love you."

"Love you too," I say.

And then, I'm gone.

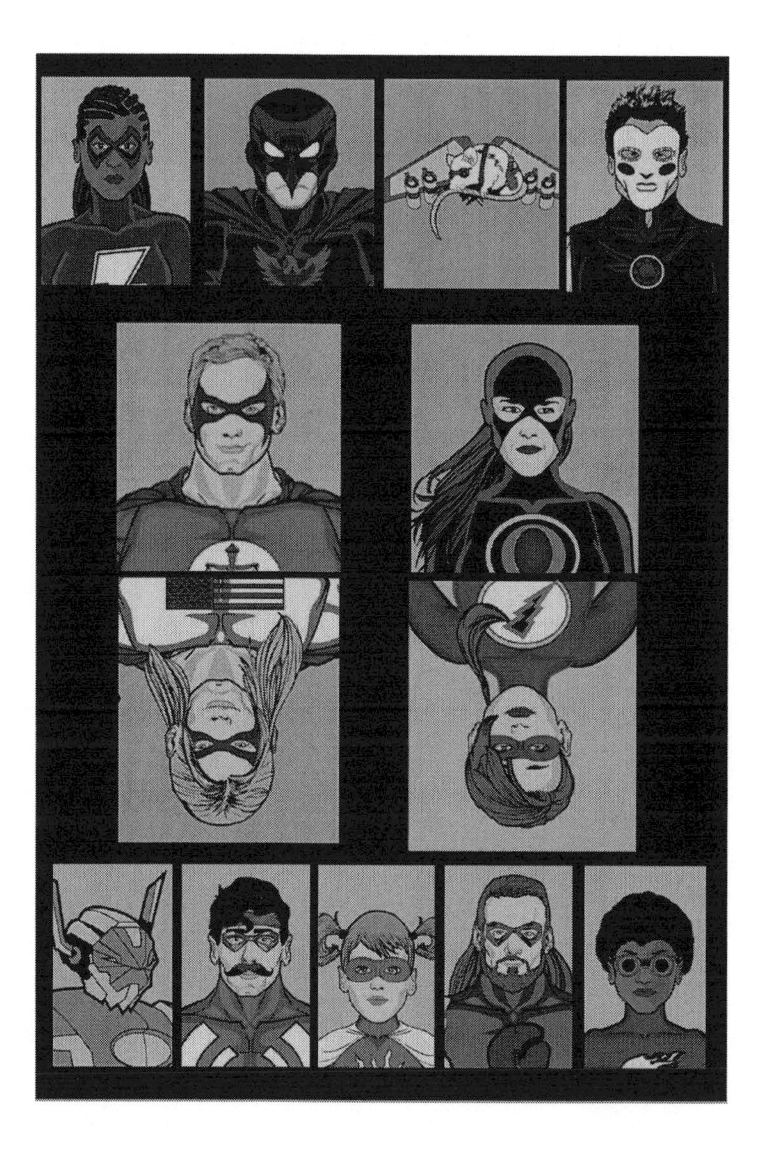

EPILOGUE

I GO BACK TO THE BEGINNING

When I open my eyes, I'm totally disoriented.

Somehow, I'm back in my bed, on the Waystation.

But how's that possible? Was I dreaming?

Then, I realize I'm holding something. It's the Time Trotter's watch! Suddenly, it all comes spinning back.

Sunbolt!

Gigi!

Meta-Taker!

The picture!

I look over at my nightstand, and the photo of my family is back! There's no crazy cat!

I drop the watch, throw off my covers, and run out of my room.

Seconds later, I crash into someone coming around the corner.

"Grace!" I yell, throwing my arms around her.

"Whoa," she says, nearly dropping her plate of jelly doughnuts. "What's gotten into you?"

"You're here!" I say. "On the Waystation!"

"Yeah, so," she says. "Did you hit your head or something? And what's up with your pajamas?"

Pajamas?

I look down to see I'm still wearing the black uniform and neon green boots I got at Groovy Threads.

"Oh," I say. "It's just a Halloween costume."

"A little early for Halloween," she says.

"Yeah," I say. "Hey, where's Mom and Dad? And Dog-Gone?"

"Some people are in the Galley," she says.

"Great!" I say, running down the hall. "Oh, and you can watch all the cat videos you want!"

"Gee, thanks," I hear her say. "Weirdo."

I book down the hall and enter the Galley. Dad and TechnocRat are having lunch at the island. I run over and give Dad a big hug.

"Hey, buddy," Dad says. "Nice to see you, too."

"Same here," I say. "By the way, the shorter hair is a huge improvement."

"Um, okay," Dad says.

Then, I pick up TechnocRat and squeeze him.

"Easy, kid," he says, dropping his cheese stick.

"I'm so sorry for earlier," I say. "I know you did everything you could to help me. You're a great hero. I just wanted you to know that."

"Aw, thanks, kid," TechnocRat says, turning red.

Then, a brown-and-black creature emerges from beneath the table.

Dog-Gone!

I run over and tackle him. We roll over each other and he licks me on the nose.

"Take it easy with him," Dad says. "He had a rough night. Apparently, someone gave him an entire bag of cookies. You wouldn't happen to know who it was, would you?"

"I'm so sorry," I say to Dog-Gone. "I promise I won't do that again, no matter how stubborn you are. You were just trying to do the right thing. I realize now it's in your nature."

Dog-Gone licks my nose again.

"Hey, where's Mom?" I ask.

"I don't know," Dad says. "She's around here somewhere. Do you want some lunch?"

"No," I say, even though my stomach rumbles.

I'm hungry, but there's something I have to do first. Apologizing to TechnocRat felt good, but it wasn't enough. I have more apologies to deliver. Lot's more.

I give Dog-Gone a belly rub, and then head out of the Galley. I make my way through the Waystation, to the one place I know I need to go.

The Hall of Fallen Heroes.

As I enter, a chill runs down my spine.

I flick on the switch, and the spotlights come on.

They're all here: Rolling Thunder, Madam Meteorite, Robot X-treme, Dynamo Joe, and Sunbolt.

But then, I'm shocked.

Because instead of five statues, there's six!

"Hey, pipsqueak," comes a familiar voice.

"Mom!"

I turn around and hug her tight.

"It's so great to see you again, Elliott," she says, rubbing my back. "I knew you'd make it home okay."

"You knew?" I ask. "But how?"

"Because it just felt right," she says. "Elliott, I know how hard this was for you, but some things are just destined to happen. It wasn't your fault Meta-Taker was created. He would have existed one way or another, and these heroes would have suffered the same fate."

I look at all of the statues.

Although I hear what Mom's saying, I can't help but feel like I failed them.

"Try not to be so hard on yourself," she says. "You did amazing things back there, but the situation had to play out the way it did. That's why I left you that note."

"Wait?" I say. "That note was from you?"

"Yes," she says. "After reading your mind in the past, I knew that one day you would need it. So, I taped it to TechnocRat's Time Warper right after you were born. But I couldn't tell you about it. Otherwise, things may have happened very, very differently."

"Wow," I say. "But how come I was the only one who wasn't affected? Why did I have to go through this?"

"I would say thank goodness it was you," she says. "But my theory is that your negation powers shielded you. At least for a while. But eventually, even time started to catch up with you. I guess the saying is true, 'time waits for no man.'"

Yeah, I guess that sort of makes sense.

Then, I get a strange thought.

"Mom, do you think it's really over?" I say. "Could this time mix-up thing happen again?"

"No," Mom says. "I think we're past this loop now. All of the things that had to happen have happened. And maybe a few things got added that were better than expected."

"You mean, like that?" I say, looking over at the sixth statue.

"I told you I'd cover your tracks," she says with a wink. "I think I accomplished that."

"Yeah, I'd say so," I answer.

"It's nice coming up here and visiting these true heroes, don't you think?" she asks.

"Yeah," I say. "I'll be coming up here more often. It feels nice to remember them."

Speaking of remembering, suddenly the image of a three-eyed man pops into my mind.

"What about Krule?" I ask.

"I don't know," she says. "We haven't heard a thing

about him since he took the Cosmic Key all those years ago."

Well, that's a relief. But then again, he's got the Cosmic Key. So, I wonder if he ever escaped from the 13th dimension? I shudder at the thought. I sure hope not, but deep down I feel unsettled just thinking about it.

"Want some lunch?" Mom asks.

"Sure," I say. "I'll be down in a few minutes."

"You got it," she says. Then, she kisses my cheek and leaves.

It's just me and the statues.

"I'm so sorry, guys," I say, tears running down my cheeks. "I-I wish I could have done more for you. But I'll never forget you. You are all a part of me now. So, whenever I do anything heroic, it'll be like we're all doing it—together."

I wipe away my tears and take one last look at the statues.

Rolling Thunder.

Madame Meteorite.

Robot X-treme.

Dynamo Joe.

Sunbolt.

The Nullifier.

Then, I flick off the lights, and head for the Galley.

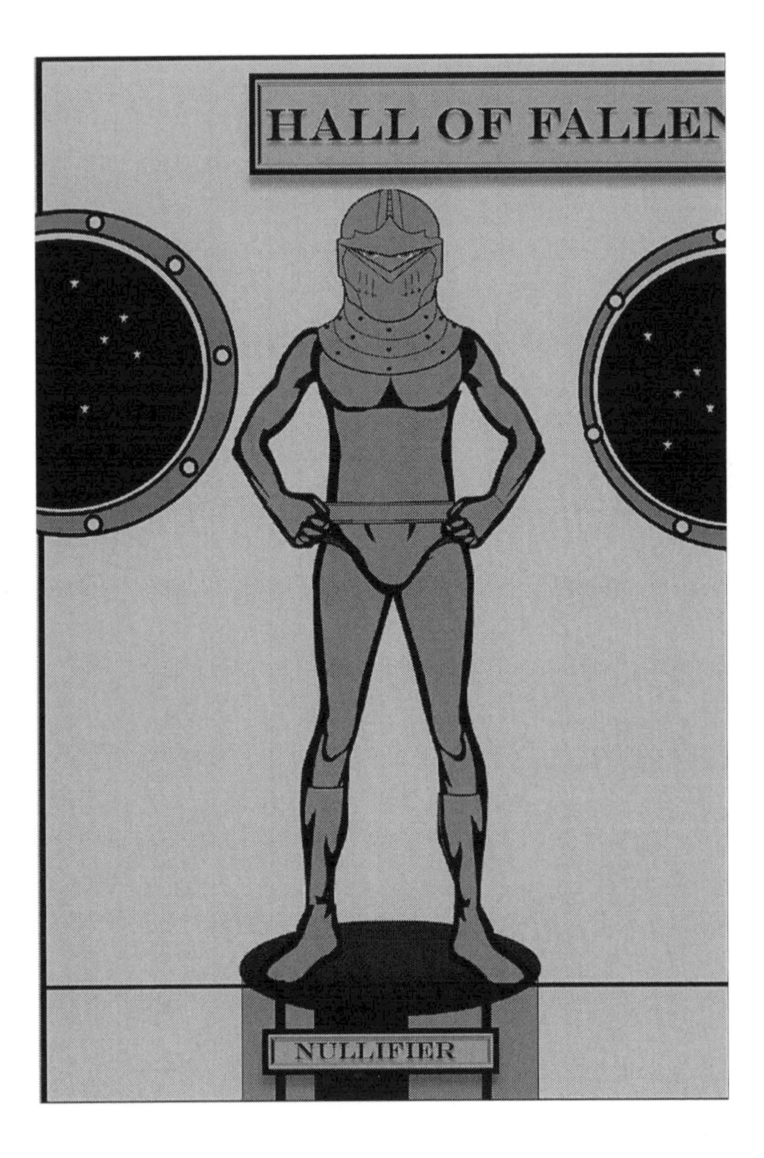
HALL OF FALLEN
NULLIFIER

EPIC ZERO 5 IS AVAILABLE NOW!

Elliott is arrested by the Intergalactic Paladins who believe he helped Krule the Conqueror escape justice. Unless Elliott can prove his innocence, he'll be banished to the dreaded 13th Dimension—forever! But when he finds out Wind Walker may be trapped in the 13th Dimension, he has no choice but to try and save him!

Get Epic Zero 5 today!

GET MORE EPIC!

Don't miss any of the Epic action!

Get a **FREE** copy of
Epic Zero Extra: Tales of a Superhero Screw Up
only at rlullman.com.

META POWERS GLOSSARY

FROM THE META MONITOR:

There are nine known Meta power classifications. These classifications have been established to simplify Meta identification and provide a quick framework to understand a Meta's potential powers and capabilities. **Note:** Metas can possess powers in more than one classification. In addition, Metas can evolve over time in both the powers they express, as well as the effectiveness of their powers.

Due to the wide range of Meta abilities, superpowers have been further segmented into power levels. Power levels differ across Meta power classifications. In general, the following power levels have been established:

- Meta 0: Displays no Meta power.
- Meta 1: Displays limited Meta power.
- Meta 2: Displays considerable Meta power.
- Meta 3: Displays extreme Meta power.

The following is a brief overview of the nine Meta power classifications.

ENERGY MANIPULATION:

Energy Manipulation is the ability to generate, shape or act as a conduit, for various forms of energy. Energy Manipulators are able to control energy by focusing or redirecting energy towards a specific target or shaping/reshaping energy for a specific task. Energy Manipulators are often impervious to the forms of energy they are able to manipulate.

Examples of the types of energies utilized by Energy Manipulators include, but are not limited to:

- Atomic
- Chemical
- Cosmic
- Electricity
- Gravity
- Heat
- Light
- Magnetic
- Sound
- Space
- Time

Note: the fundamental difference between an Energy Manipulator and a Meta-morph with Energy Manipulation capability is that an Energy Manipulator does not change their physical, molecular state to either generate or transfer energy (see META-MORPH).

FLIGHT:

Flight is the ability to fly, glide or levitate above the Earth's surface without use of an external source (e.g. jetpack). Flight can be accomplished through a variety of methods, these include, but are not limited to:

- Reversing the forces of gravity
- Riding air currents
- Using planetary magnetic fields
- Wings

Metas exhibiting Flight can range from barely sustaining flight a few feet off the ground to reaching the far limits of outer space.

Often, Metas with Flight ability also display the complimentary ability of Super-Speed. However, it can be difficult to decipher if Super-Speed is a Meta power in its own right or is simply a function of combining the Meta's Flight ability with the Earth's natural gravitational force.

MAGIC:
Magic is the ability to display a wide variety of Meta abilities by channeling the powers of a secondary magical or mystical source. Known secondary sources of Magic powers include, but are not limited to:

- Alien lifeforms
- Dark arts
- Demonic forces
- Departed souls
- Mystical spirits

Typically, the forces of Magic are channeled through an enchanted object. Known magical, enchanted objects include:

- Amulets
- Books
- Cloaks
- Gemstones
- Wands
- Weapons

Some Magicians have the ability to transport themselves into the mystical realm of their magical source. They may also have the ability to transport others into and out of these realms as well.

Note: the fundamental difference between a Magician and an Energy Manipulator is that a Magician typically channels their powers from a mystical source that likely requires use of an enchanted object to express these powers (see ENERGY MANIPULATOR).

META MANIPULATION:
Meta Manipulation is the ability to duplicate or negate the Meta powers of others. Meta Manipulation is a rare Meta power and can be extremely dangerous if the Meta Manipulator is capable of manipulating the powers of multiple Metas at one time. Meta Manipulators who can manipulate the powers of several Metas at once have been observed to reach Meta 4 power levels.

Based on the unique powers of the Meta Manipulator, it is hypothesized that other abilities could include altering or controlling the powers of others. Despite their tremendous abilities, Meta Manipulators are often unable to generate powers of their own and are limited to manipulating the powers of others. When not utilizing their abilities, Meta Manipulators may be vulnerable to attack.

Note: It has been observed that a Meta Manipulator requires close physical proximity to a Meta target to fully manipulate their power. When fighting a Meta Manipulator, it is advised to stay at a reasonable distance and to attack from long range. Meta Manipulators have been observed manipulating the powers of others up to 100 yards away.

META-MORPH:

Meta-morph is the ability to display a wide variety of Meta abilities by "morphing" all, or part, of one's physical form from one state into another. There are two sub-types of Meta-morphs:

- Physical
- Molecular

Physical morphing occurs when a Meta-morph transforms their physical state to express their powers. Physical Meta-morphs typically maintain their human physiology while exhibiting their powers (with the exception of Shape Shifters). Types of Physical morphing include, but are not limited to:

- Invisibility
- Malleability (elasticity/plasticity)
- Physical by-products (silk, toxins, etc…)
- Shape-shifting
- Size changes (larger or smaller)

Molecular morphing occurs when a Meta-morph transforms their molecular state from a normal physical state to a non-physical state to express their powers. Types of Molecular morphing include, but are not limited to:

- Fire

- Ice
- Rock
- Sand
- Steel
- Water

Note: Because Meta-morphs can display abilities that mimic all other Meta power classifications, it can be difficult to properly identify a Meta-morph upon first encounter. However, it is critical to carefully observe how their powers manifest, and, if it is through Physical or Molecular morphing, you can be certain you are dealing with a Meta-morph.

PSYCHIC:

Psychic is the ability to use one's mind as a weapon. There are two sub-types of Psychics:

- Telepaths
- Telekinetics

Telepathy is the ability to read and influence the thoughts of others. While Telepaths often do not appear to be physically intimidating, their power to penetrate minds can often result in more devastating damage than a physical assault.

Telekinesis is the ability to manipulate physical objects with one's mind. Telekinetics can often move objects with their mind that are much heavier than they could move physically. Many Telekinetics can also make objects move at very high speeds.

Note: Psychics are known to strike from long distance, and, in a fight, it is advised to incapacitate them as quickly as possible. Psychics often become physically drained from extended use of their powers.

SUPER-INTELLIGENCE:
Super-Intelligence is the ability to display levels of intelligence above standard genius intellect. Super-Intelligence can manifest in many forms, including, but not limited to:

- Superior analytical ability
- Superior information synthesizing
- Superior learning capacity
- Superior reasoning skills

Note: Super-Intellects continuously push the envelope in the fields of technology, engineering, and weapons development. Super-Intellects are known to invent new approaches to accomplish previously impossible tasks. When dealing with a Super-Intellect, you should be mentally prepared to face challenges that have never been encountered before. In addition, Super-Intellects can come in all shapes and sizes. The most advanced Super-Intellects have originated from non-human creatures.

SUPER-SPEED:
Super-Speed is the ability to display movement at remarkable physical speeds above standard levels of speed. Metas with Super-Speed often exhibit complimentary abilities to movement that include, but are not limited to:

- Enhanced endurance
- Phasing through solid objects
- Super-fast reflexes
- Time travel

Note: Metas with super-speed often have an equally super metabolism, burning thousands of calories per minute, and requiring them to eat many extra meals a day to maintain consistent energy levels. It has been observed that Metas exhibiting Super-Speed are quick thinkers, making it difficult to keep up with their thought process.

SUPER-STRENGTH:

Super-Strength is the ability to utilize muscles to display remarkable levels of physical strength above expected levels of strength. Metas with Super-Strength are able to lift or push objects that are well beyond the capability of an average member of their species. Metas exhibiting Super-Strength can range from lifting objects twice their weight to incalculable levels of strength allowing for the movement of planets.

Metas with Super-Speed often exhibit complimentary abilities to strength that include, but are not limited to:

- Earthquake generation through stomping
- Enhanced jumping
- Invulnerability
- Shockwave generation through clapping

Note: Metas with Super-Strength may not always possess this strength evenly. Metas with Super-Strength have been observed to demonstrate powers in only one arm or leg.

META PROFILE CHARACTERISTICS

FROM THE META MONITOR:

In addition to having a strong working knowledge of a Meta's powers and capabilities, it is also imperative to understand the key characteristics that form the core of their character. When facing or teaming up with Metas, understanding their key characteristics will help you gain deeper insight into their mentality and strategic potential.

What follows is a brief explanation of the five key characteristics you should become familiar with. **Note**: the data that appears in each Meta profile has been compiled from live field activity.

COMBAT:

The ability to defeat a foe in hand-to-hand combat.

DURABILITY:

The ability to withstand significant wear, pressure or damage.

LEADERSHIP:

The ability to lead a team of disparate personalities and powers to victory.

STRATEGY:

The ability to find, and successfully exploit, a foe's weakness.

WILLPOWER:

The ability to persevere, despite seemingly insurmountable odds.

ABOUT THE AUTHOR

R.L. Ullman is the bestselling author of the award-winning EPIC ZERO series and the award-winning MONSTER PROBLEMS series. He creates fun, engaging page-turners that captivate the imaginations of kids and adults alike. His original, relatable characters face adventure and adversity that bring out their inner strengths. He's frequently distracted thinking up new stories, and once got lost in his own neighborhood. You can learn more about what R.L. is up to at rlullman.com, and if you see him wandering around your street please point him in the right direction home.

For news, updates, and free stuff, please sign up for the Epic Newsflash at rlullman.com.

ACKNOWLEDGMENTS

I need to give a major shout out to my personal team of Meta heroes for helping me with this story. Thanks to my wife, Lynn, for her story smarts and editing skills. Thanks to my son, Matthew, for his story ideas and encouragement to keep the series going. And thanks to my daughter, Olivia, for her unwavering support. I would also like to thank you for supporting Elliott and his super family.

YOU CAN MAKE A BIG DIFFERENCE

Calling all heroes! I need your help to get Epic Zero 4 in front of more readers.

Reviews are extremely helpful in getting attention for my books. I wish I had the marketing muscle of the major publishers, but instead I have something far more valuable, loyal readers just like you! Your generosity in providing an honest review will help bring this book to the attention of more readers.

So, if you've enjoyed this book, I would be very grateful if you could spare a minute to leave a review on the book's Amazon page. Thanks for your support!

Stay Epic!

R.L. Ullman

DO YOU HAVE MONSTER PROBLEMS?

Some Monsters are Meant to be Heroes…

Readers' Favorite Book Award Winner

Life bites for a misfit kid who discovers he's the last vampire alive and must save the world from evil monsters in this funny, award-winning series for kids 9-12!

Get Monster Problems today!

Made in the USA
Monee, IL
13 November 2019